REMEMBER US THIS WAY

SOUND OF US BOOK 1

C.R. JANE

Remember Us This Way by C. R. Jane

Copyright © 2019 by C. R. Jane

All rights reserved.

For permissions contact:

crjaneauthor@gmail.com

This book is a work of fiction. Names, characters, businesses, places, events, locales, and incidents are either the products of the author's imagination or used in a fictitious manner. Any resemblance to actual persons, living or dead, or actual events is purely coincidental.

For all the girls who dared to be happy.

THE SOUND OF US SERIES

Remember Us This Way
Remember You This Way
Remember Me This Way

JOIN C.R. JANE'S READERS' GROUP

Stay up to date with C.R. Jane by joining her Facebook readers' group, C.R.'s Fated Realm. Ask questions, get first looks at new books/series, and have fun with other book lovers!

https://www.facebook.com/groups/C.R.FatedRealm

REMEMBER US THIS WAY SOUNDTRACK

"Always Remember Us This Way"-
Lady Gaga

"Naked"-
James Arthur

"Something's Gotta Give"-
Camila Cabello

"Love in the Dark"-
Adele

"Bad Liar"-
Imagine Dragons

"Leave a Light On"-
Tom Walker

"Perfect"-
One Direction

"Adore You"-
Miley Cyrus

BLURB

They are idols to millions worldwide. I hear their names whispered in the hallways and blasted through the radio. Their faces are never far from the television screen, tormenting me with images of what I gave up.

To everyone else, they're unattainable rockstars, the music gods who make up The Sound of Us. But to me? They'll always be the boys I lost.

I broke all our hearts when I refused to follow them to L.A., convinced I would only bring them down. Years later, after I've succumbed to a monster, and my life has become something out of a nightmare, they are back.

I'm no longer the girl they left behind. But what if I've become the woman they can't forget?

When the sun goes down
    And the band won't play
    I'll always remember us this way

-Lady Gaga, Always Remember Us This Way

PROLOGUE
BEFORE

According to the Sounds of Us Wikipedia page, the band hit almost instant stardom as soon as they finished recording their first album. A small indie band that had gained only regional notoriety, Red Label had taken a huge risk by signing them. The good looks and the killer voices of the three band members combined with the chance at a larger platform ended up making Sounds of Us the Label's most successful band in history. They released their first album, Death by Heartbreak, in 2013, and the first single, Follow You Into the Dark, made it to the Billboard Top 100 immediately.

It was their second single that propelled Sounds of Us to legend status though. Cold Heart was number one on the charts almost the second it was released. That led to four other songs ending up in the top ten. Three of them reached number one, with a fourth hitting number two on the charts. That album was torture in its finest form for me. Partly because I had lost them, but also partly because every one of those songs was about me. And that was just the hits. There were a lot more references in the songs that never got released as singles

It was a sharp stab in the chest to hear songs blaring from radios – songs whose lyrics contained exact words each of them had said to me, and that I had said to them.

And while some of the songs were wistful and pained, others were angry. Pissed-off. Occasionally enraged. It was uncomfortable. Actually, it was excruciating. At least for the first couple of months. I stopped listening to music eventually, something that had meant the world to me my entire life. I just couldn't handle the reminder of them anymore. My heart couldn't take it.

But every so often, a car would go by with its window down, or I'd walk past a motel room playing the radio, and I'd hear one of their voices and it would be an unexpected jolt of pain all over again.

After the release of their album, the band embarked on a short European tour, then followed it up with a much larger American tour. They started selling out stadiums. They appeared on every late-night show there was. Everyone wanted a piece of them. They were like this generation's Beatles, probably even bigger. The next two albums certainly were bigger, although those were easier for me to listen to since the songs about me faded as time went on. They were the most celebrated band in the world and there was no sign of their success slowing down anytime soon. It was everything they had ever dreamed about and that I had dreamed about with them.

They lived up to the bad boy image their label wanted to sell. Rumors of drug use and rampant women kept the gossip sites busy. I tried to ignore the magazines in the store racks by the checkout stand, but some of the pictures of the guys stumbling out of clubs with five girls each were a little too damning to be completely unfounded. And of course, there were the rumors that Tanner had secretly been in and out of rehab for the last two years in between tours. Tanner had always struggled with addiction but had only dabbled in hard drugs when I knew him. It wasn't hard for me to picture him struggling with them now that he probably had easy access to whatever he wanted from people desperate to please them all.

I often wondered if any part of the boys I knew were still around after I let myself give into my own addiction of catching up on any Sounds of Us news I could find. And then I would hear about them buying a house for someone who had lost everything in a natural disaster or hear of them participating in a charity drive to keep a no-kill shelter up and running, and I would know that a part of them was still there.

I've never made peace with letting them go. I never will.

I hear the song come on from the living room. I had forgotten I had read that they were performing for New Year's Eve tonight in New York City before they embarked on their North American tour for the rest of the year. I wanted to avoid the room the music was coming from, but not even my hate for its current occupant could keep my feet from wandering to where the song was playing.

As I took that first step into the living room, and I saw Tanner's face up close, my heart clenched. As usual, he was singing to the audience like he was making love to them. When the camera panned to the audience, girls were literally fainting in the first few rows if he so much as ran his eyes in their direction. He swept a lock of his black hair out of his face, and the girls screamed even louder. Tanner had always had the bad boy look down perfectly. Piercing silver eyes that demanded sex, and full pouty lips you couldn't help but fantasize over, he was every mother's worst nightmare and every girl's naughty dream. I devoured his image like I was a crack addict desperate for one more hit. Usually I avoided them like the plague, but junkies always gave in eventually. I was not the exception.

"See something you like?" comes a cold, amused voice that never ceases to fill me with dread. I curse my weakness at allowing myself to even come in the room. I know better than this.

"Just coming to see if you need a refill of your beer," I tell him nonchalantly, praying that he'll believe me, but knowing he won't.

My husband is sitting in his favorite armchair. He's a good-looking man according to the world's standards. Even I have to admit that despite the fact that the ugliness that lies inside his heart has long prevented me from finding him appealing in any way. His blonde hair is parted to the side perfectly, not a hair out of place. Sometimes I get the urge to mess it up, just so there can be an outward expression of the chaos that hides beneath his skin.

After I let the guys go, there was nothing left for me in the world. Instead of rising above my circumstances and becoming someone they would have been proud of, I became nothing. Gentry made perfectly clear that anything I was now was because of him.

Echoes of my lost heart beat inside my mind as another song starts to play on the television. It's the song that I know they wrote for me. It's angry and filled with betrayal, the kind of pain you don't come back from. The kind of pain you don't forgive.

Too late I realize that Gentry just asked me something and that my silence will tell him that I'm not paying attention to him. The sharp strike of his palm against my face sends me flying to the ground. I press my hand to my cheek as if I can stop the pain that is coursing through me. I already know this one will bruise. I'll have to wear an extra layer of makeup to cover it up when Gentry forces me to meet him at the country club tomorrow. After all, we wouldn't want anyone at the club to know that our lives are anything less than perfect.

The song is still going and somehow the pain I hear in Tanner's voice hurts me more than the pain blossoming across my cheek. Would it not hurt them as much if they knew everything I had told them to sever our connection permanently was a lie? Would they even care at this point that I had done it to set them free, to stop them from being dragged down into the hell I never seemed to be able to escape from? At night, when I lay in bed, listening to the sound of Gentry sleeping peacefully as if the world was perfect and monsters didn't exist, I told myself that it would matter.

"Get up," snaps Gentry, yanking me up from the floor. I'm really off my game tonight by lingering. Nothing makes Gentry madder than when I "wallow" as he calls it. As I stumble out of the room, my head spinning a bit from the force of the hit, a sick part of me thinks it was worth it, just so I could hear the end of their song.

LATER THAT NIGHT, long after I should have fallen asleep, my mind plays back what little of the performance I saw earlier. I wonder if Jensen still gets severe stage fright before he performs. I wonder if Jesse still keeps his lucky guitar pick in his pocket during performances. I wonder who Tanner gets his good luck kiss from now.

It all hurts too much to contemplate for too long so I grab the Ambien I keep on my bedside table for when I can't sleep, which is often, and I drift off into a dreamland filled with a silver eyed boy who speaks straight to my soul.

The next morning comes too early and I struggle to wake

up when Gentry's alarm goes off. Ambien always leaves me groggy and I haven't decided what's better, being exhausted from not sleeping, or taking half the day to wake up all the way.

Throwing a robe on, I blurrily walk to the kitchen to get Gentry's protein shake ready for him to take with him to the gym.

I'm standing in front of the blender when Gentry comes up behind me and puts his arms around me, as if the night before never happened. I'm very still, not wanting to make any sudden movement just in case he takes it the wrong way.

"Meet me at the club for lunch," he asks, running his nose up the side of my neck and eliciting shivers...the wrong kind of shivers. He's using his charming voice, the one that always gets everyone to do what he wants. It stopped working on me a long time ago.

"Of course," I tell him, turning in his arms and giving him a wide, fake smile. What else would my answer be when I know the consequences of going against Gentry's wishes?

"Good," he says with satisfaction, placing a quick, sharp kiss on my lips before stepping away.

I pour the blended protein shake into a cup and hand it to him. "11:45?" I ask. He nods and waves goodbye as he walks out of the house to head to the country club gym where he'll spend the next several hours working out with his friends, flirting with the girls that work out there, and overall acting like the overwhelming douche that he is.

I don't relax until the sound of the car fades into the distance. After eating a protein shake myself (Gentry doesn't approve of me eating carbs), I start my chores for the day before I have to get ready to meet him at the country club.

My hands are red and raw from washing the dishes twice. Everything was always twice. Twice bought me time and ensured there wouldn't be anything left behind. An errant fleck of food, a spot that hadn't been rinsed – these were things he'd notice.

Hours later, I've vacuumed, swept, done the laundry, and cleaned all the bathrooms. Gentry could easily afford a maid, but he likes me to "keep busy" as he puts it, so I do everything in this house of horrors. I repeat the same things every day even though the house is in perfect condition. I would clean every second if it meant that he was out of the house permanently though.

I straighten the pearls around my neck and think for the thousandth time that if I ever escape this hell hole, I'm going to burn every pearl I come across. I'm dressed in a fitted pastel pink dress that comes complete with a belt ordained with daisies. Five years ago, I wouldn't have been caught dead in such an outfit but far be it for me to wear jeans to a country club. I slip into a pair of matching pastel wedges and then run out to the car. I'm running late and I can only hope that he's distracted and doesn't realize the time.

As I drive, I can't help but daydream. Dream about what it would have been like if I had joined the guys in L.A. Bellmont is a sleepy town that's been the same for generations. I haven't been anywhere outside of the town since I got married except to Myrtle Beach for my honeymoon.

The town is steeped in history, a history that it's very proud of. The main street is still perfectly maintained from the early 1900s, and I've always loved the whitewashed look of the buildings and the wooden shingles on every roof. The town attracts a vast array of tourists who come here to be close to the beach. They can get a taste of the coastal southern flavor of places like Charleston and Charlotte, but they don't have to pay as high of a price tag.

It's a beautiful prison to me, and if I ever manage to escape from it, I never want to see it again.

I turn down a street and start down the long drive that leads to Bellmont's most exclusive country club. The entire length of the road is sheltered by large oak trees and it never ceases to make me feel like an extra in Gone With the Wind whenever I come here. The feeling is only reinforced when I pull up to the large, freshly painted white plantation house that's been converted into the club.

My blood pressure spikes as I near the valet stand. Just knowing that I'm about to see Gentry and all of his friends is enough to send my pulse racing. I smile nervously at the teenage boy who is manning the stand and hand him my keys. He gives me a big smile and a wink. It reminds me of something that Jesse used to do to older women to make them swoon, and my heart clenches. Is there ever going to be a day when something doesn't remind me of one of them?

I ignore the valet boy's smile and walk inside, heading to the bar where I can usually find Gentry around lunch time. I pause as I walk inside the lounge. Wendy Perkinson is leaning against Gentry, pressing her breasts against him, much too close for propriety's sake. I know I should probably care at least a little bit, but the idea of Gentry turning his attentions away from me and on to Wendy permanently is more than I can even wish for. I'm sure he's fucked her, the way she's practically salivating over him as he talks to his friend blares it loudly, but unfortunately that's all she will ever get from him. Gentry's obsession with me has thus far proved to be a lasting thing. But since I finally started refusing to sleep with him after the beatings became a regular thing, he goes elsewhere for his so-called needs when he doesn't feel like trying to force me. At least a few times a week I'm assaulted by the stench of another woman's perfume on my husband's clothes. It's become just another unspoken thing in my marriage.

Martin, Gentry's best friend, is the first to see me and his eyes widen when he does. He coughs nervously, the poor thing thinking I actually care about the situation I've walked into. Gentry looks at him and then looks at the entrance where he sees me standing there. His eyes don't widen in anything remotely resembling remorse or shame...we're too far past that at this point. He does extricate himself from Wendy's grip however to start walking towards me, his gaze devouring me as he does so. One thing I've never doubted in my relationship with Gentry is how beautiful he thinks I am.

"You're gorgeous," he tells me, kissing me on the cheek and putting a little too much pressure on my arm as he guides me to the bar. Wendy has moved farther down the bar, setting her sights on another married member of the club. It's funny to me that in high school I had wanted to stab her viciously when she set her sights on Jesse, but when she actually sleeps with my husband I could care less.

"My parents are waiting in the dining hall. You're ten minutes late," says Gentry, again squeezing my arm to emphasize his displeasure with me. I sigh, pasting the fake smile on my face that I know he expects. "There was traffic," I say simply, and I let him lead me to the dining hall where the second worst thing about Gentry is waiting for us.

Gentry's mother, Lucinda, considers herself southern royalty. Her parents owned the largest plantation in South Carolina and spoiled their only daughter with everything that her heart desired. This of course made her perhaps the most self-obsessed woman I had ever met, and that was putting it lightly. Gentry's father, Conrad, stands as we approach, dressed up in the suit and tie that he wears everywhere regardless of the occasion. Like his son, Gentry's father was a handsome man. Although his hair was slightly greying at the temples, his face remained impressively unlined, perhaps due to the same miracle worker that made his wife look forever thirty-five.

"Darling, you look wonderful as always," he tells me, brushing a kiss against my cheek and making we want to douse myself in boiling water. Conrad had no qualms about propositioning his son's wife. I couldn't remember an interaction I'd had with him that hadn't ended with him asking me to sneak away to the nearest dark corner with him. I purposely choose to sit on the other side of Gentry, next to his mother, although that option isn't much better. She looks me over, pursing her lips when she gets to my hair. According to her, a proper southern lady keeps her hair pulled back. But I've never been a proper lady, and the guys always loved my hair. Keeping it down is my silent tribute to them and the person I used to be since everything else about me is almost unrecognizable.

Lucinda is a beautiful woman. She's always impeccably dressed, and her mahogany hair is always impeccably coiffed. She's also as shallow as a teacup. She begins to chatter, telling me all about the town gossip; who's sleeping with who, who just got fake boobs, whose husband just filed for bankruptcy. It all passes in one ear and out the other until I hear her say something that sounds unmistakably like "Sounds of Us."

I look up at her, catching her off guard with my sudden interest. "Sorry, could you repeat that?" I ask. Her eyes are gleaming with excitement as she clasps her hands delicately in front of herself. She waits to speak until the waiter has refilled her glass with water. She slowly takes a sip, drawing out the wait now that she actually has my attention.

"I was talking about the Sounds of Us concert next week. They are performing two shows. Everyone's going crazy over the fact that the boys will be coming home for the first time since they made it big. It's been what...four years?" she says.

"Five," I correct her automatically, before cursing myself when she smirks at me.

"So, you aren't immune to the boys' charms either..." she says with a grin.

"What was that, Mother?" asks Gentry, his interest of course rising at the mention of anything to do with me and other men.

"I was just telling Ariana about the concert coming to town," she says. I hold my breath waiting to hear if she will mention the name. Gentry's so clueless about anything that doesn't involve him that he probably hasn't heard yet that they're coming to town.

"Ariana doesn't like concerts," he says automatically. It's his go-to excuse for making sure I never attend any social functions that don't involve him. Ariana doesn't like sushi. Ariana doesn't like movies. The list of times he's said such a thing go on and on. I feel a slight pang in my chest. Ariana. Gentry and his family insist on calling me by my full name, and I miss the days where I had relationships that were free and easy enough to use my nickname of Ari.

"Of course she doesn't, dear," says Lucinda, patting my hand. The state of my marriage provides much amusement to Lucinda and Conrad. Both approve of the Gentry's "heavy hand" towards me and although they haven't witnessed the abuse first hand, they're well aware of Gentry's penchant for using me as a punching bag. Gentry's parents are simply charming.

I pick at my salad and listen to Lucinda prattle on, my interest gone now that she's off the subject of the concert. Gentry and his dad are whispering back and forth, and I can feel Gentry shooting furtive glances at me. I know I should be concerned or at least interested about what their talking about, but my mind has taken off, thinking about the fact that in just a few days' time, the guys will be in the same vicinity as me for the first time in five years. If only….

"Ariana," says Gentry, pulling me from my day dream. I immediately pull on the smile I have programmed to flash whenever I'm in public with Gentry.

"Yes?"

"I think you've had enough to eat," he tells me as if he's talking about the weather and not the fact that he's just embarrassed me in front of everyone at the table.

I shakily set my fork down, my cheeks flushing from his comment. I was eating a salad and I'm already slimmer than I should be. But Gentry loves to control everything about me, food being just one of many things. I see Lucinda patting her lips delicately as she finishes eating her salmon. My stomach growls at the fact that I've had just a few bites to eat. I have a few dollars stashed away in my car, I'll have to stop somewhere and grab something to eat on the way home. That is if Gentry doesn't leave at the same time as me and follow me.

When I've gotten my emotions under control, I finally lift my eyes and glance at my husband. He's back in deep conversation with Conrad, their voices still too soft for me to pick anything up. Looking at him, I can't help but get the urge to stab him with my silverware and then run screaming from the room. The bastard would probably find a way to haunt me from the grave even if he didn't survive. Still, I find my hand clenching involuntarily as if grasping for a phantom knife.

After that one terrible night when it became clear that I couldn't go to L.A. to meet up with the guys, I was lost. I got a job as a waitress and was living in one of those pay by week extended stay motels since there was no way I could stay in my trailer with *them* anymore. I met Gentry Mayfield while waitressing one night. He was handsome and charming, and persevered in asking me out even when I refused the first half a dozen times. My heart was broken, how could I even think of trying to give my broken self to someone else? I finally got tired of saying no and went on a date with him. He made me smile, something that I didn't think was possible, and every date after that seemed to be more perfect than I deserved. I didn't fall in love with Gentry, my heart belonged to three other men, but I did develop admiration and fondness for Gentry in a way that I hadn't thought possible. After pictures started to surface on the first page of the gossip sites of the guys with hordes of beautiful women, and the fact that my life seemed to be going nowhere, marrying Gentry seemed to be the second chance that I didn't deserve. Except the funny thing about how it all turned out is that my life with Gentry turned out worse than I probably deserved, even after everything that had happened.

Three months after we were married, I burnt dinner. Gentry had come home in a bad mood because of something that had happened at work. Apparently, me burning dinner was the last straw for him that day and he struck me across the face, sending me flying to the ground. Afterwards, he begged and pleaded with me for forgiveness, saying it would never happen again. But I wasn't stupid, I knew how this story played out. I stayed for a week so that I could get ahold of as much money as I could and then I drove off while he was at work. I was stopped at the state lines by a trooper who evidently was friends with Gentry's family. I was dragged kicking and screaming back home where Gentry was waiting, furious and ready to make me pay. Every semblance of the man that I had thought I was marrying was gone.

I had $5,000 to my name when I met him. I'd gotten it from selling the trailer that I inherited when my parents died in a car crash after one of their drunken nights out on the town. Gentry had convinced me that I should put it in our "joint account" right after we got married and stupidly, I had agreed to do it. I never got access to that account. Gentry stole my money, he stole my self-esteem. No, he didn't steal it, he chipped away at it and just when I thought I'd crumble, he kissed me and cried over me and told me he'd die without me.

I tried to get away several more times, by bus, on foot, I even went to the police to try and report him. But the Mayfield's had everyone in this state in their pocket, and nothing I said or did worked. I eventually stopped trying. It had taken me a year of not running away to get my car back and to be able to do things other than stay home, locked in our bedroom, while Gentry was at work.

Gentry stood up from the table, bringing me back to the present. A random song lyric floated through my mind about how the devil wears a pretty face, it certainly fit Gentry Mayfield.

"I'm heading to the office for the rest of the day. What are your plans?" he asks, as if I had a choice in what my plans were.

"Just finishing things around the house and going to the store to get a few ingredients for dinner," I tell him, waving a falsely cheerful goodbye to Gentry's parents as he walks me out of the dining area towards the valet stand. We stop by the exit and he pulls me towards him, stroking the side of my face that I've painted with makeup to hide the bruise he gave me the night before. My eyes flutter from the rush of pain but Gentry somehow mistakes it as the good kind of reaction to his touch. He leans in for a kiss.

"You're still the most beautiful woman I've ever seen," he tells me, sealing his lips over mine in a way that both cuts off my air supply and makes me want to wretch all at once. I hold still, knowing that it will enrage him that I don't do anything in response to his kiss, but not having it in me to fake more than I already have for the day. He pulls back and searches my eyes for something, I'm not sure what. He must not find it because his own eyes darken, and his grip on my arms suddenly tightens to a point that wouldn't look like anything to a club passerby, but that will inevitably leave bruises on my too pale skin.

He leans in and brushes his lips against my ear. "You're never going to get away from me, so when are you going to just give in?" he spits out harshly. I say nothing, just stare at him stonily. I can see the storm building in his eyes.

"Don't bother with dinner, I'll be home late," he says, striding away without a second glance, probably to go find Wendy and make plans to fuck her after he leaves the office, or maybe it will be at the office knowing him.

I wearily make my way through the doors to the valet stand and patiently wait for my keys. It's a different kid this time and I'm grateful he doesn't try to flirt with me.

On my way back from the country club I find myself taking the long way back to the house, the way that takes me by the trailer park where I grew up. I park by the office trailer and find myself walking to the field behind the rows of homes. Looking at the trash riddled ground, I gingerly walk through the mud, flecks of it hitting the formerly pristine white fabric of my shoes. I walk until I get to an abandoned fire pit that doesn't look like it's been used for quite a while. For probably five years to be exact.

I sit on a turned over trash barrel until the sun sits precariously low in the sky and I know that I'm playing with fire if I dare to stay any longer. I then get up and walk back to my car, passing by the trailer I once lived in. It's funny that after everything that has happened, at the moment I would give anything to be back in that trailer again.

2

THEN

Trailer Park Trash. That's what I've been called all my life and when I moved to Bellmont, South Carolina, I didn't expect it to be any different. The fact that the police had to be regularly called on my parents regardless of where we moved always ensured that my reputation was soured in just a few weeks. Like usual, Terry and David, my good for nothing mother and step-father, got into a knockout fight within a week of us moving, the day before I was supposed to start my new school in fact. Fueled by alcohol and whatever drugs they had been able to get their hands on that night; the screaming and shouting roused all the neighbors. Which is a bit hard to do in most trailer parks since the residents are usually used to the out of the ordinary. The fact that my parents sounded like they were going to murder each other always pushed the residents to call the police. No one wanted a dead body on their hands.

When I heard the sirens, I snuck out my bedroom's window. I didn't want to be around just in case they forgot to put their drugs away before letting the police inside. It was best if the police didn't know that the two psychopaths had a child. Dealing with the CPS right when I was starting a new school was not something I wanted to experience.

The air was chilly despite the mugginess of the night, and I pulled my threadbare sweater tightly around myself to try and keep warm. I walked through the rows of trailers. Some were kept up nicely and you knew that even though the residents inside may not have very much money, they still took pride in their possessions. Others were like my own place, barely staying put together. Rusted and decaying, just like its residents.

The chaos of my upbringing had spurred me to be almost fanatically the opposite from my parents. Where they were dirty, I was clean, almost unhealthily so. Terry's cigarette smoke would leak under my door if I didn't block it out, and just even walking through the front door of our place made me feel gross since they never bothered to clean up after themselves after one of their binges that left sticky spilled liquor and discarded food everywhere. I would rush back to my room, close the door, and block the bottom with a wet towel. Then, I would start cleaning, wiping every surface down, until all I could smell was the harsh lemon scent of my cleaning spray. I repeated this process every day and even now, while walking in the dark, I felt the urge to be wiping down my room, wiping away the despair of my life.

After walking around for a while, the flicker of a fire in the distance caught my eye. Even knowing that I should head back to my room and see if the police were gone so I could try and get a good night's rest for my first day at my new school, curiosity got the better of me. I began to walk towards the fire. The sound of male and female voices and laughter from people who sounded close to my age spurred me on even more.

There are two buildings on one side of the fire, and I

approach from that side so I can just look and hopefully not be seen. There are two boys sitting on turned over steel drums, both with girls wrapped around them. The flames light up their faces and even in the dim lighting I can tell that they're beautiful. The most beautiful boys I've ever seen in fact. Boys might not be the right word for them though. If anything, they look closer to men than they do boys. I watch entranced as their hands move over the girls' bodies. The two girls, both beautiful as well with the same uniform of shorts that border on indecency, and tops cut off half way across their stomach, seem enthralled and I don't blame them. I'm feeling a bit enthralled myself. I feel like a voyeur as the guy whose blonde hair seems to shine like the sun under the fire's reflection pulls his red headed girl in for a kiss that looks far better than the ugly, awkward ones that I've experienced in my life.

A third boy walks in from the woods with a naughty look on his face, holding the hand of a gorgeous blonde girl. He murmurs something in her ear as I watch and she smiles, her face blushing at his words. His midnight colored hair is a little too long, swept back carelessly off his face. It fits the 'don't give a fuck' vibe he has going as he looks at the scene in front of him, perusing it indifferently. I feel the insane urge to run up and drag my hands through it, just to see if it's as soft as it looks. He leads the girl to another seat and pulls her to sit in his lap. One of his friends pulls away from his girl long enough to murmur something at him and he throws back his head to laugh. I smile watching it, it's not often that I see someone whose laugh takes over their whole body. I find myself wanting to know what the blonde guy said to make his friend laugh like that. The two girls in their laps aren't laughing so I wonder if it's some kind of inside joke. I've never been close enough to anyone to have an inside joke.

The boy who came in from the woods turns to the girl in

his lap and starts making out with her. I take a step closer to the fire unwittingly, and immediately curse myself when the boy's eyes open and he stares right at me. He hesitates for a moment when our eyes lock, and then he continues to kiss the girl, albeit a little more distractedly. He turns his head, casting more light from the fire on his face than before.

With the extra light shining on him, the first thing I notice about him are his eyes. They are a remarkable silver color that I've never seen before. They practically glow in the dark making him look more like ethereal prince than teenage boy. At least I think he's a teenage boy. I could tell as he was walking that he's tall. Far taller than my 5'7 frame. He's also big, much bigger than the boys I've seen before. He looks like he spends the perfect amount of time working out, not too much, not too little...just right.

Crap, I'm now thinking in terms of nursery rhymes. I really need to get out more. I focus in on the gorgeous specimen in front of me again and although he's still kissing the lucky wench in his arms, his eyes are amused as he watches me. He finally pulls away and murmurs something to the other two gorgeous creatures. They stop what they're doing and their eyes flash towards me as well. I'm frozen in their gazes. I've never felt such intensity focused on me before.

I finally snap out of it and twirl around, almost tripping on a bag of trash that's fallen open on the ground as I hurry away. I can hear the sound of the girls' laughter as I run, and my face is ablaze with color even though there's no one to witness what I just did. I don't stop running until I get to the outside of the trailer. Peeking around the side of it, I see that the front drive is blissfully empty of any police. I walk around to the outside of my bedroom's window. Lifting it up, I stick my head in and listen carefully to see if I hear Terry or David. It's blissfully quiet. Terry and David are either asleep or they've been taken away by the police. Hopefully that's not the case as I still need a place to live for two more years. Despite their horribleness, they have somehow been able to keep a roof over our heads for the most part. There's only a couple of times when we had to sleep in our car until David could scrounge up enough money to get us somewhere. It's not an experience I would like to experience again.

I climb into my room and shut the window, clicking the lock shut even though it's so flimsy it won't actually prevent anyone from coming into my room. Although being honest with myself, if any of those three guys had followed me to my trailer, I wouldn't exactly be kicking them out of my room. Not that they would be interested in me when they had those girls to play with. I shake my head at my foolishness. I need to take a shower after my sprint through the humid, soupy South Carolina night, but I don't know what waits for me beyond my bedroom door. I'll just have to go to bed sweaty and hope to shower in the morning before school.

The last thought before I fall asleep is what it felt like when those pair of silver eyes watched me in the dark.

MY ALARM CLOCK blares and jars me from a jumble of dreams. I turn it off and lay there for a second, trying to get my bearings. My brain finally wakes up enough to realize that I need to get ready for school or I'm going to be late for my first day. I grab my things and crack open the door. I creep down the hall to see if Terry or David are anywhere to be seen. The door of their room is open, and I peer through, feeling a mixture of relief and disgust when I see both of them sprawled out all over each other on their bed, beer cans littered on the carpet from the bender they must have had after the police left.

I hurry and shower, content that they are going to leave me alone for at least this morning. Once I'm finished, I look through the meager offering of clothes I have in my closet. I pull out a pleated black skirt and a white blouse that I picked up at a second hand store the week before. I'm not sure what kids wear here, but at my other school the students were always dressing nicely. I can always grunge up tomorrow if I find that it isn't the case here.

There's no money for lunch and I know that I'll have to suck it up and fill out the form for free student lunch if I don't want to have to starve for the rest of the year. It's bad enough that I'm going to have to start school in the middle of the fall semester, but having the other students stare and make fun of the fact that I'm on the free lunch program will I'm sure be the icing on the cake.

I walk out the door after realizing how late it has gotten and how long it is going to take me to walk to school. I walk along the main road that runs past the trailer park since I haven't figured out any back roads to get to the school yet. I've just about made it to the school when a shiny, white convertible comes racing past me, flicking me with pieces of mud from the storm the day before. I stare in disgust at my now brown speckled white blouse and curse my luck and my life. I start to jog despite the risk of getting sweaty in hopes that I can wipe myself off before the bell rings.

As I walk through the parking lot, I pass the white sports car that ruined my day. I can't help but admire it, it's easily the most expensive car that I've ever seen, like something out of a movie. Looking around the parking lot, I realize that it's full of expensive looking cars. How in the world did a trailer park end up being in the same school district as the kids who can afford a parking lot full of Mercedes?

The driver of the white convertible gets out. All I can see is a mess of black hair until he turns around and I see that it's one of the guys from last night. He stares at me intensely for a second with those silver eyes, but I'm quicker this morning at coming to my senses than I was last night, and I finish walking into the school.

I'm lucky that most of the mud came out of my top, but now there are slightly see through splotches all over my white blouse from where I rubbed wet paper towels on it to get the mud off. Trying to remedy the situation, I pull my thick brunette hair to the front of my body. I'm just finishing up when the door of the bathroom swings open. Continuing my luck for the day, two of the girls from the night before walk in laughing loudly with each other. They are both wearing cheer-leading uniforms today that actually manage to show almost as much of their bodies as their outfits the night before did. They pass by me disinterestedly, and I let out a sigh of relief. At least they didn't see me watching them make out with their boyfriends or it was too dark for them to recognize me. I hurry and make my escape once they walk into their stalls.

I just manage to grab my schedule from the front office and find my class right as the bell is ringing. As I walk into my first class, History, I can feel the eyes of everyone in the room upon me. It doesn't help that the teacher stops on my name during roll and has me stand up and say my name and a fun fact about me. Standing up, I don't make eye contact with anyone. After introducing myself, I'm at a loss for what to say. I live in a trailer park? I call my parents by their first names because they're perpetually strung out?

"One fact about you now," the teacher says gently, finally sensing that I'm not the type of student that loves getting up in the front of the class.

I blurt out the first stupid thing that comes to my mind. "There's nothing interesting about me."

There's a shocked silence after I sit down and even the teacher looks taken aback. I feel like an utter and complete lunatic. What a way to start off my time at a new school. I'm sure everyone thinks I'm a complete freak now. I keep my head down, not wanting to see the disgusted looks on my new classmates' faces. The teacher luckily recovers quickly from my comment and starts to launch into a lecture about the Revolutionary War. I tune out a bit since my old school covered the Revolutionary War a month ago. It's warm in the room and a little stuffy. I find myself falling asleep as the teacher drones on until the door to the classroom opens up about halfway through class and everyone in the room seems to sit up a little straighter in their desks, their eyes locked on the door and the gorgeous guy that just walked through it.

"Well, Mr. Carroway, thank you for deciding to grace us with your presence," says the teacher in a voice that's trying to come across annoyed, but instead sounds bemused as if she can't quite help herself.

"You know I would never miss your class," says a deep male voice, laced with seduction. It's the kind of voice that says he knows how to give a girl a good time. Or at least it's how I would imagine that kind of voice sounds.

I look up, my cheeks blazing just from the sound of his voice, and I see him. Boy, do I see him. The gorgeous creature that just walked through the door oozes masculinity, the kind you don't see in boys my age. The faint scruff on his chin and cheeks, the longish, wavy, carelessly unkempt blonde hair, the incredible blue and expressiveness of his eyes rimmed in long dark lashes, a firm jaw line-he's the whole package and I realize suddenly that he was one of the boys from the night before. I duck my head back down, hoping that he won't see me, but not before I notice his pouty lips that look like they were made for kissing.

I hear footsteps walking closer to me and then past me, and then the sound of him sitting in the desk right behind me. I can feel his eyes on the back of my head, and I find myself suddenly wondering if the back of my head is attractive, which is crazy since I've never once worried about that before. Not sure how it suddenly became the only thing I can think about.

The class settles down although I can see that none of them are able to keep their eyes from straying to the seat behind me every few minutes. It's like they are compelled to keep him in their sights. Which I don't exactly blame them for. I've found myself wishing that he was sitting somewhere that I could see him instead of behind me. I can feel his warm breath lightly blowing on the back of my neck and I wonder why he's leaning so close to me.

A few minutes pass and the teacher resumes her lecture. I suddenly feel a tap on my shoulder. I flinch, not knowing what I should do. When I don't turn immediately around, I feel the tap again. I turn my head to look at him.

"Hi," he says, as if we aren't in the middle of class. He gives me an expectant look like I'm supposed to be answering him back. There's recognition in his eyes as he looks over my face. It's like he's memorizing every freckle.

"Hi," I whisper back, and then start to turn back around since I'm expecting the teacher to say something any minute now.

"Did you see something you liked last night, pretty girl?" he whispers, his rough, deep voice sending chills down my spine...the good kind of chills. The comment annoys me since I don't like to be played with, so I turn all the way back around in my seat in a huff. I'm shocked when I feel him take some strands of my hair and start to play with them. Who does this guy think he is? I lean forward, trying to give him a hint, but he ignores me and keeps playing with my hair.

When the bell finally rings and the teacher stops lecturing, I realize that I've let this stranger play with my hair for over an hour. I turn around to look at the offender, but I find that he's already gathered his books and is walking by me, winking at me as he passes by. He leaves the room without saying anything to me, leaving a mess of sighs and yearning girls behind him.

"Isn't he perfect?" comes a giggling, dreamy sounding voice. I look to the right of me and see a cheerful looking auburn-haired cheerleader standing next to me. She's not the redhead from the night before thank goodness. I give her a questioning look, wondering why she's talking to me.

"You're new here, right?" she asks. "That was quite the interesting fact you gave about yourself," she says with a giggle. When I still don't say anything, she starts to look unsure of herself. I sigh to myself. Might as well be friendly.

"Yes, I just moved here," I tell her finally, and her shoulders relax as I finally answer her. She walks beside me as I exit the classroom.

"I bet you didn't have boys like that where you came from," she says, gesturing to where the blonde-haired god is getting something out of his locker, surrounded by a crowd of admirers. As if he heard her, he looks straight at us, giving me a smirk like he's seen me undressed.

"Oh my gosh," the cheerleader next to me squeals. "He likes you!"

"Sorry, what's your name?" I ask, confused why this girl is still walking next to me. She blushes at my question.

"Whoops, guess I forgot that. My name is Amberlie," she says. "I'm on the cheerleading team," she tells me as if I'm blind and somehow missed the fact that she's wearing her uniform.

"Never would have guessed," I say dryly and then flinch at the embarrassed look on her face. I'm not sure why I'm being so rude to the first person in a while that has actually been nice to me.

"I'm sorry. I'm no good at this," I tell her.

"Good at what?" she asks, tilting her head as she examines me.

"Being a friend," I answer, and a smile lights up her face.

"Good thing I'm really good at it," she says, linking her arm through mine and walking with me down the hall to my next class while she gossips about random people standing in the hallway. She happens to have calculus, my next class, with me, and we sit down in desks next to each other. Looking around, I'm disappointed that the guy from my first class doesn't seem to be in this one. Although considering that he didn't show up for history until it was half way over, there's still a chance he could be in the class.

Leaning over, I finally ask the question I've been dying to know since I saw him. "Who was that guy?" I ask Amberlie, who is now painting her nails a bright red as we talk.

She looks up and grins, her face somehow managing to be even more animated than it already was.

"You mean that yummy sex god in History?" she asks with a smirk. I roll my eyes but nod at her description.

"That was Jesse Carroway. One of 'The Three'," she says with a sigh, her eyes going dreamy as she says his name. She says "the three" as if it's an official title.

"One of the three?" I ask, thinking of the other two guys from last night.

She's about to answer me when the teacher walks in. This teacher has a severe looking face and an aura about her that says she doesn't put up with nonsense. Seeing as how the room went silent and Amberlie has quickly put away her nail polish, I figure it's not a good time to ask any more questions. The class drags on and I can tell by the end that it's going to be the class I like least of all. Watching paint dry would probably be more interesting than what the teacher just put us through. When the bell finally rings, the whole class lets out a sigh of relief and hurries out of the classroom all at once. Amberlie starts chattering about something the moment she is able and I'm trying to listen, but I'm distracted by another of the most attractive men I've ever seen making his way down the hall. The hordes of students part down the middle as he walks through them. He has a haughty look on his face like no one around him is good enough to hold his attention.

And maybe no one is good enough. The guy walking down the hall is . . . Holy snickerdoodle. I swallow the breath stuck in my throat. Broad, powerful shoulders taper to a narrow waist and long legs. He towers over most of the students he passes. His light brownish-blonde hair is tousled in a carefree way that's impossible to mimic. An etched jaw and sparkling green eyes make the package even more delectable.

"You don't get used to it," Amberlie says, letting out another one of the wistful sighs that I'm beginning to expect from her. We watch as the green-eyed stunner is joined by the sex god that I now know goes by Jesse. "It's a miracle the two of them don't burn the building down with their hotness," she says, and I completely agree. They definitely did not make guys who looked like that back in Ohio where I lived before.

"What's his name?" I find myself whispering, unable to talk loudly through the lust that's building inside of me.

"Jensen Reid," she says in that same dreamy tone that she used when she talked about Jesse.

"And what's the name of the third one?" I ask, sure that it's the guy that gave me wet dreams from last night.

"Tanner Crosby," she says. "I really never could choose between any of them. I want them all."

I laugh at her pronouncement, not disagreeing with her. I have to force myself not to go down my imagination's road of what exactly having all of them would entail.

I watch the guys as they meet up with the girls I recognize from the night before. Jensen's cold eyes soften as soon as he narrows his focus on his girl. He caresses the girl's cheek, a hint of a smile tugging at the corner of his full mouth. He bends to the girl's ear, whispering until a flush races across her chest. Her hand lands on his neck, holding him in place. The scene is intimate and almost too indecent to watch, yet I can't look away. I inexplicably want that to be me that's holding his attention. He waits while she says something only he can hear, finally dragging his gaze to someone down the hallway. His eyes brush by me and he freezes. There's a look in his eyes that's hard to decipher. It's hot and sinfully intrusive. He takes his time looking me up and down, the girl standing right by him, begging for attention, now an afterthought. He says something to Jesse that has the whole group looking over at me. Not wanting to catch the brunt of their attention any longer I hurry away, only to run into what feels like a boulder.

"Uumph," I groan as I start to fall to the ground from the impact. A strong pair of arms catch me right before I land. I look up so I can see the face of whoever just saved me, and I immediately want the ground to swallow me up into oblivion. It's the silver-eyed, perfect specimen from the night before-the one who caught me ogling him while he made out with his girl.

"Tanner Crosby," I whisper, and then immediately want to knock myself out. He's totally going to think I'm a stalker now.

The smile that breaks on his face is easy, surprising me, and if his wide eyes are an indication, it appears to catch him off-guard as well.

"Princess, you keep calling me by my full name and I'm going to get a god complex. Like a god, I change lives, but it's just Tanner. Or sir, if you're so inclined. Now how about dinner?"

I blink rapidly at him. So off guard that I don't know what to say. I open my mouth but instead of words coming out, it flops like a fish.

"Torturing the new girl?" comes a voice that makes me want to be even farther in the ground. I look up into Jesse's amused face, his blue eyes searing into me. I realize at that moment that Tanner is still holding me, and I wrench myself out of his grasp, my skin tingling where he was touching me. Jensen decides to make an appearance at that moment, and I find myself standing in the middle of them. There's a faint buzzing sound in my ears as I feel the weight of their stares on me. It makes me feel somehow small, but at the same time empowered to have their attention.

"What's your name, sweetheart?" asks Jensen. Hearing his voice for the first time, I'm struck with how smooth it is. It's much more charming than I would have guessed since out of the three of them, he has a somewhat menacing air about him. Studying him while he waits for an answer, I notice his brilliant white teeth and full lips, the light stubble that covers his angular jaw. I find myself leaning towards him like a crazed lunatic. I notice that his eyes aren't the green I originally thought, but green with a dark ring of brown in the center. What does me in is the single dimple that appears on his right cheek when he smiles suddenly.

"Did you forget?" he whispers, invading my personal space to the point where I take a step back, right into Tanner.

"Forget what?" I ask, my mind mush under the circumstances. He leans in again until I'm practically sandwiched between the two of them. I can feel Jesse's mocking smile as he watches the scene play out. I can't believe that this is happening in the hallway, with what feels like a million people watching us, and no one has stepped in.

"Your name," says Tanner from behind me, his lips brushing against my ear, sending shocks coursing all over my body.

It's a weird thing the fact that I have these three enormous men around me, all of which could easily overpower me. And I feel strangely safe. Like I'm where I belong. Shaking off the dangerous thought, I squeeze myself from between them and start to walk down the hallway to my next class. I turn around when I'm far enough away not to be caught up in their spell. "Ariana," I tell them with a wink that portrays far more confidence than I possess.

The next class passes in a blur. I come back to life when the bell for lunch rings. I've always hated lunch at new schools. Especially starting in the middle of the semester. Everyone has their spots and people all picked out. Which means I'll end up either eating in the bathroom or at a table in the corner since no one will know me.

I walk into the enormous lunch room and just like I predicted, all the tables are full of bustling students who all know their place and where they fit into the hierarchy of the school. However, unlike other lunchrooms that I've seen, this one isn't built around the football team or the basketball team. It's built around *them*.

As a little girl, I'd been fascinated watching how the moths outside our trailer would swarm the front light at night. Watching how the entire lunch room swarmed around Jensen, Tanner, and Jesse felt like I was watching the same thing. They sat at a table in the middle of the room, lounging in their seats as if they were gods playing with their mortal subjects. Two of the girls from last night were sitting at the same table, but I noticed in an annoyingly satisfied way, that the guys didn't seem to be paying them any attention. Instead they were huddled together, discussing something that everyone in the room seemed to want to know about.

Taking a deep breath, I walk into the lunchroom. I keep my head down even though I can feel the eyes of people drilling holes into the sides of my head. Perusing the options in the lunch line I'm dismayed to see that it's just as bad as what I'm used to in school cafeterias. But I'm not going to turn down a free lunch. As I grab a slice of pizza and a salad and walk to the register, I say a silent prayer that the cafeteria worker won't make a big deal out of me being in the free lunch program.

I get up to the register and am just about to open my mouth to tell her my lunch number when a Dr. Pepper and a Snickers gets plopped on my tray and a $10 bill gets thrown at the shocked cafeteria worker. Before I can even look at my bene- factor an arm leads me back into the cafeteria room where literally everyone's eyes are now on me. I look up and I'm shocked to see that Jesse is the one who has his arm around me.

He looks down at me, an impish twinkle in his eye. "I'm just showing you to the seat we saved for you."

My mouth is frozen open and I'm unable to form words. Hopefully this reaction of mine isn't something that's going to continue indefinitely. I'm sure they would start to think I wasn't right in the head if I never could say anything to them.

Jesse never moves his arm, even after he sits me down on the bench in between him and Jensen. After I set my tray down, he grabs the Dr. Pepper and somehow manages to smoothly open it with one hand.

I'm not sure what's going on, so I do what I do best. Put my head in the sand and start to eat my salad while not making eye contact with anyone. No one talks to me, which doesn't bother me at all. The guys chat over my head as if there's nothing strange about the new girl sitting right in the middle of them. I happen to glance up while getting a drink of water and I see Amberlie making signals at me from a table across the way where she's sitting with the football team and a bunch of other cheerleaders. She's pretending to hyperventilate, and I struggle to hold in a smile about how ridiculous she looks.

"What's making you smile like that, pretty girl?" whispers Jesse into my ear, sending a cascade of tingles down my whole body. I ignore his question but turn to look at him.

"What am I doing here?" I whisper.

"What do you mean?" he asks innocently.

"I mean...why am I sitting at your table right now? You don't even know me."

A kid across the table with jet black hair and a pierced eyebrow overhears our conversation and decides to pipe in. "Because he or one of the others wants to fuck you, obviously new girl," he says.

I stare at him shocked, wanting to stand up and eat in the bathroom at this point.

"Tyson, feel free to leave the table," says Jensen calmly. I think he's joking but obviously goth boy doesn't because his face starts to pale.

"Dude, seriously..." he begins, before Jensen speaks again.

"Don't make me ask you twice," he says in that same calm voice which I'm beginning to realize actually sounds so scary because it's so calm. It's like Jensen is lying in wait, trying to trick his prey into relaxing before he attacks.

Muttering to himself, goth boy aka Tyson, grabs his tray and throws the whole thing into the trash before stomping out of the room. The whole lunch room gets quiet after that, everyone eyeing our table warily. I realize that whatever just happened disrupted an established group and everyone is feeling a little out of sorts.

Finding bravery from somewhere, I turn to Jensen and Tanner. "So, was he right? Am I sitting here because you want to fuck me?" I ask. Both of them look a little shocked at my question, but Jesse starts laughing hysterically beside me. Tanner is the first to recover and he gives me a smooth, cool grin that takes my breath away for a second.

"Of course he's right, Princess. Have you seen yourself?" he asks. "But I'm beginning to believe you're not going to make it easy for us."

His honesty knocks me over and I can't think of anything to say. So, I continue eating. My nerves are jumping so much though that I can't taste anything, and I feel like my skin is randomly twitching as I sit there. I feel pulling on my hair and I realize that Jesse has started to play with my hair like he did in History this morning. It catches me off guard at how touchy Jesse is considering he doesn't know me. Even Jensen is sitting way too close to me for comfort. His leg is pressed up against mine, feeling far more intimate than I'm sure it's intended. He's just a big guy. All of them are.

The guys continue to talk around me, occasionally saying something to the people around us who are literally salivating to get any kind of scrap from them. Looking around at the rest of the table, everyone is beautiful. But they all pale in comparison to *them*.

When the bell rings, I realize that I haven't eaten half of my food. Which is definitely unlike me since heaven knows if Terry and David will have any food for us to eat at home.

When they do have cash, they prefer to spend it on liquid nourishment rather than actual food.

I pull out the schedule I was given this morning to see where I'm off to next. Before I can get a good look at it, it's swiped out of my hands. I look up annoyed and see that Tanner is studying it.

"Yep, you've got class with me next, Princess," he says, taking my hand and pulling me up. Jesse grabs my tray off the table and slips the Snickers in my pocket before walking away.

Tanner doesn't let go of my hand until we're in class and I'm seated with him next to me. I've been touched more today than I have my entire life I realize. I feel uncomfortable and itchy thinking about it, but at the same time I want more of it. I need more of it.

I try to listen as our English teacher begins to talk about Great Expectations, the book that the class is currently reading. It's hard to concentrate however since Tanner has taken my hand and is now drawing doodles on the back of it. I try to pull it away, but he doesn't give it back. Instead he smiles infuriatingly while pretending not to notice my efforts.

By the time the bell rings I'm convinced that I'm going to fail all my classes if any of the guys are in there. It's a good thing that I've actually read Great Expectations at my old school or that pop quiz the teacher gave us at the end of class would have gone totally different. I'm not going to be so lucky next time. I see Amberlie down the hallway and lift my hand to wave, but she squeaks and runs away when she sees that Tanner is still walking next to me.

I finally turn to Tanner. "Ok, what gives? Is this some kind of lead up to a hazing ritual for the new girl? You guys have barely spoken a word to me all day but you're buying me lunch, having me sit with you, sitting next to me in class... What are you planning?"

Once again, he boxes me into the lockers and I have to keep my eyes averted because I'm becoming convinced that his silver ones are capable of casting spells since I act like a fool whenever I look into them.

"Princess," he says softly. I make the mistake of glancing up, and I wish I didn't when Tanner's teeth sink into his bottom lip. The air crackles with tension between the ten inches separating his mouth from mine. Shit. My pulse speeds up, and I'm sure if he looks close enough he'll see it pounding in my throat. His gaze narrows into something not at all friendly, but scorching and predatory and nothing but heat. I'm hot with a newfound flush. He shakes. A tremble crosses his shoulders, and his eyes lose their crisp clarity for a snapshot in time. I push back so fast that I slam my head against the lockers, creating a loud bang that leaves people staring at us once again.

"Why do you keep calling me Princess?" I ask in an unsteady voice while staring steadfastly at his still too near lips.

"Because you're as pretty as what I imagine a princess would look like," he says. I scoff. "That's the corniest line I've ever heard," I tell him.

He leans in, whispering his lips across my ear. "It's not a line," he says before pushing back from me and striding away.

My legs shake all the way to my next class which is blissfully empty of any of them. My traitorous heart wishes otherwise though.

3
NOW

I haven't been able to get the concerts out of my head ever since Lucinda mentioned it. It doesn't help that Sounds of Us songs are on constant repeat as the area ramps up for the concerts. Most of the radio stations have been advertising contests to get tickets to the sold out shows and my whole body has been twitching all day as I try to hold myself off from trying to enter one.

Days of this torture finally have worn me down and I find myself holding my phone, my palms sweating, as I listen to a radio DJ announce another contest. This one complete with backstage passes. There's no way that I'll win, but I suddenly can't prevent myself from hovering above the phone keys.

"Alright, it's the moment you've all been waiting for, Caller 87 gets backstage passes to the Sounds of Us concert tomorrow night. All you have to do is call 1-800-254-KDIN. On your mark get set go!" the announcer crows.

I'm frozen for a moment in indecision and then my fingers are flying across my phone, typing in the radio station number that I've memorized from hearing the announcement for over a week. I hold my breath as the phone starts to ring. An automated voice tells me I'm number 52 so I hurriedly hang up and call again. This time it rings through.

"Congratulations you're Caller 87! What's your name?"

I hesitate, not understanding how this happened. I never win. I'm literally the unluckiest person on the planet as amply shown by the current state of my life.

"Ari," I say with a stutter, choking on my name as if I've never said it before.

"Well Ari, how do you feel right now?" the announcer asks in that charming smooth voice that all radio DJs seem to possess.

The truth was I felt scared, nauseous, and weak at the moment, but I knew I couldn't tell him that. "Excited," I finally say in a voice that sounds about as far from excited as you can get. The interview is a little awkward after that since I'm not giving the announcer very much to work with. He finally finishes the interview and sends me to someone who collects my personal information for the tickets. I give a sigh of relief as I end the call.

I drive home in a daze, completely forgetting to drop off the clothes that Gentry needed to be dry cleaned. I hurriedly hide them in the trunk of my car, so Gentry doesn't notice them when he gets home. I walk into the house and immediately head to the kitchen where I know I should be starting dinner. My mind is in a daze though. This doesn't feel like real life at the moment. I'm trembling as I set my phone down on the counter.

I hear the garage door open just as I start to think about what I'm going to do. I flinch. There's obviously no way that I'm going to be able to make up an excuse good enough to leave the house for the night. Gentry likes to know where I am at all times or there are severe consequences. I rub my still bruised cheek absentmindedly. I'm very familiar with Gentry's consequences.

The sound of feet hitting the wood floor makes my muscles seize in awareness, my stomach turns over in revulsion.

"Ariana," calls Gentry from the hallway where he's just come in from the garage. I panic as he starts to walk towards the kitchen. I hurry and erase the numbers of the radio stations from my call log knowing that he'll check my phone first chance he gets to see who I have talked to today. I've just set the phone down and walked over to the fridge to pretend like I'm preparing dinner when he walks in. I feel his shadow fall over my right shoulder. His heavy footsteps rock the floor beneath my feet as he approaches. I smell his cologne when he leans over my shoulder.

"Why didn't you answer me?" he asks in an annoyed voice.

"I was trying to think of what to make for dinner and spaced out," I tell him with a laugh that hopefully conveys "silly girl" rather than "I'm hiding something from you."

He frowns, but let's it go. I try not to cringe when he slides a kiss across my cheek. He of course makes no effort to avoid the bruised side and I swear there's a triumphant glint in his eye when I flinch from the pressure he puts on the injury. He cages me into the counter for a long moment. I feel a trickle of sweat slide down my spine. He hums, the vibration right by my ear and I swallow the bile that rises up into my mouth. The humming. He knows that I know what the humming signifies. I grit my teeth together.

"I'll put together some chicken and rice. It will be quick," I tell him, desperate to distract him. I keep my eyes averted knowing that he likes for me to appear cowed in his presence. Meeting his eyes would present a challenge, a challenge that would only encourage him. I didn't want his plans to include his favorite activity. He was a creature of habit: dinner, then television, then something to drink, then an attempt at me.

He slides two fingers down my back, over my tee shirt, pausing just before he reaches the top of my jeans. He enjoys this game, teasing me with the threatening promise of later. He loves holding all the power in this exchange.

"How about we go out?" he says. I look at him suspiciously. Gentry likes a schedule. For as long as I can remember Friday and Saturday have been nights we go out to eat. It's Wednesday.

"You want to go out?" I ask stupidly.

"I have that business trip this weekend, so I thought we would celebrate our anniversary early," he says, wrapping his arms around me.

I had completely forgotten about his trip. I had also completely forgotten about our anniversary. When you hate something so much, things like anniversaries don't mean very much. I would probably remember my anniversary from now on however since the concert was that night. It's like the universe has decided to smile at me all at once. I'll be home alone all weekend. I won't have to worry about getting away from Gentry.

The thought brings a smile to my face. It's a genuine smile and I realize that Gentry's taken aback by my happiness, thinking that it has to do with us celebrating our anniversary. I'm not going to tell him differently.

"Go get a pretty dress on, sweetheart," he says, trying to take advantage of the mood he thinks I'm in by going in for a kiss. Determined to keep him happy and off any potential scent of my plans for the weekend, I go with it, wanting to gag the whole time. I deliberately hide my face from him as I turn to go get dressed since I know that the look on my face is anything but pleasant.

Standing in my closet, I flip through the options, my mind going to what I'm going to wear to the concert instead of what I'm supposed to be picking out for dinner. I'm disgusted at the options in my closet. So much pink, so much paisley print. My jewelry box isn't any better since it's full of pearls. I can't go to the concert looking like I just stepped off the stage of a southern beauty pageant. Gentry diverts my attention back to looking for a dress to wear for dinner when he yells up the stairs for me to hurry. I quickly grab a fitted pink cocktail dress that I know Gentry favors and I change. Squaring my shoulders, I coach myself that I can put on the show of the century tonight if it means getting to go to the concert tomorrow night.

Walking down the stairs, I pull at the strand of pearls around my neck. Gentry gave them to me last anniversary and I can't help but think that they feel like a collar. The feeling is only reinforced by the possessive, satisfied look he always gets when I wear them. The pearls are a symbol of his ownership of me, and I hate them. If I ever get the chance to escape from this god-forsaken place, I'll never wear a pearl again.

As we drive to one of the nicest steakhouses in town, Gentry chatters about some deal he's just signed to turn a plot of land right outside the city limits into a new shopping center. I realize while he's talking that the plot of land is the trailer park I grew up in. My emotions are so complicated about that place. The best and some of the very worst moments of my life have happened there, but it's almost like I need the trailer park to keep on existing so I don't forgot those memories. Right now, I can drive past when I need to and remember how Tanner's eyes felt on me that first night. I can remember where Jesse first really kissed me, where Jensen first told me I was beautiful. It's stupid but if I lose where those events happened, it feels like it could erase that they actually happened at all.

"Is there some other land you can do it on?" I ask abruptly, knowing that I've made a huge mistake as soon as the words come out of my mouth. Gentry hates to be reminded of my origins. If it were up to him, he would have burned the whole park to the ground years ago. He tells everyone that doesn't know me that my parents are wealthy business owners in Georgia. I remember the first time that he introduced me like that, how bad I felt that my fiancée was so ashamed of me. But then of course he's done far worse things to me since then, and I almost feel silly that I was upset about that in the first place.

"And why would you care about what happens to that cess-pool?" he asks in a cold, deadly voice that always represents trouble for me. I hesitate, knowing that if I push this it could somehow ruin the upcoming freedom I'm planning on. He could end up deciding to take me on his business trip with him. Despite the pang in my chest, I tell him that I don't care and that the shopping center sounds lovely. I don't say another word for the rest of the drive as I listen to him continue to talk about the mall.

We walk into the restaurant and I'm reminded why Gentry always wants to come here on special occasions. It's always crowded with the "who's who" of Bellmont. He puts his arm around my waist and struts to our table giving a wink to a pretty waitress as we pass by. Throughout dinner I'm forced to put up with his over the top display of affection as he makes clear to the whole town who I belong to. I idly think that if it were any of the guys in the place of Gentry right now, I would probably be enjoying it. I would like the idea that they wanted to show me off or wanted to show everyone that I was theirs.

I get more and more nervous as dinner passes. Gentry has consumed quite a bit of bourbon and his hands are roving even more than before. He's starting to hum that little tune that always makes me want to throw up, making it clear what he's going to expect when he gets home... and I just can't. I can't do it. Any time that I've slept with him since we've been married has only been because I feared reprisals and Gentry usually doesn't try to cross the line of forcing me. Hence why he had started fucking half the town. But tonight seemed different. It seems silly, but somehow if I let Gentry touch me tonight, I won't be able to go to the concert. I'll feel like I'm somehow tainted even more than I normally am.

So I order him another drink. Although I go out of my way to not feed Gentry's ego, tonight I go overkill. We talk on and on about how wonderful he is, how handsome he is, how smart he is. And through it all he continues to drink until he's almost comatose. Satisfied that he won't be trying anything tonight and will probably be incapacitated for most of tomorrow before he leaves for his trip, I call for the check and drive us home. Helping him into bed and hearing him snore as he immediately falls into a deep sleep, I let my mind wander to the weekend. I barely sleep the entire night as I think about seeing them again.

4

THEN

'm walking to school the next morning when an enormous black truck pulls up next to me. It rolls down a window, I'm sure the occupants of the truck expecting me to come up to it. I'm street smart enough to know that's how girls get kidnapped however, and I start to jog to try and get away. The truck drives slowly next to me.

"Pretty girl, do you want a ride?" Jesse asks, sticking his head out the window and wiggling his eyebrows in a way that lets me know he would love to give me two different kinds of rides. It starts sprinkling at that moment and considering I'm foolishly wearing a white shirt again, it seems like it would be stupid to not take the ride. Besides, I still need to figure out why they seem so interested in me.

I sigh and open the door, having to hoist myself up in order to get into the truck since it's so tall. "Compensating much?" I ask dryly, and a laugh barks out of him as if he wasn't expecting it.

"My dad actually bought this for me," he says ruefully, and I wonder what it would be like for your parents to actually buy you things or really even remember that you're supposed to go to school at all. "But no, it matches the package quite well," he says with a cocky wink. And I roll my eyes while thinking that there's something really attractive about his easy-going personality and perfect smile. He seems to be not weighed down by the world, which is a rare trait in someone.

We chat about random things like our weird mutual love for the Patriots and all things Tom Brady and before I know it, we're pulling into the school parking lot.

"Stay there," he says suddenly, hopping out of the truck effortlessly and jogging over to my door. He opens it and picks me up, sliding my body down his before setting me down. I'm once again flustered and gaping like a codfish while he looks like he just won the lottery.

He slings an arm over my shoulders as I've noticed he likes to do, and he leans into me. "You're going to get used to me touching you a lot, pretty girl," he says, and I don't even try to answer. Who are these guys?

Suddenly he snorts and I look up at him to see what he finds so funny. He's looking down the sidewalk and I see that Jensen is walking towards us, looking like he just got done going for a jog. There's a light sheen of sweat over his golden skin and his t-shirt is sticking to him, showcasing the very defined six-pack that he's rocking. It makes extremely clear how perfectly muscular he actually is. His hair looks thick and soft with a slight wave that gives it body, and it's slightly mussed like he just ran his hands through it. In short, he looks absolutely delicious.

He comes near us, staring at me in that intense way that he has.

"'Show-off," Jesse mutters from beside me.

Jensen furthers the show by suddenly taking his shirt off and using it to wipe his face. I'm rewarded with the view of a wall of smooth, tanned skin. Broad shoulders frame his wide chest that tapers into a trim waist. His pecs bulge over a set of rippling abs that transcend into sexy V muscles that disappear under his waistband. His body resembles something out of the romance books that Terry likes to read twenty-four seven. I think I need to borrow Jensen's shirt to wipe off the drool that is most likely coming out of my mouth.

"Down girl," whispers Jesse and I turn and glare at him, unable to give him a good one since he's so freaking hot as well.

Jensen and Jesse talk for a minute about an assignment they have for a class I'm not in, neither of them really saying anything to me. I'm content with that. I've always been awkward with chit-chat and for once it feels comfortable to listen instead of feeling pressure to say something.

"I'm going to go shower," says Jensen finally, reaching over to sweep a strand of my hair behind my ear. He turns towards me first, slowly catching my body on fire as his eyes skim me from my head to my feet. "Your shoe's untied," he says suddenly. "Hold still."

Mesmerized, I do as he says and watch as he kneels in front of me. Still shirtless, I track his lean, sinewy muscles as they stretch and flex in front of me in a tantalizing dance. He's close enough to touch. I want to lean in and lick every hard ridge of his body. It's literally torture to stand this close to him. He stands up and shoots me a lazy grin that somehow tells me he knows the effect he's having on me right now. I find myself licking my lips as I watch him walk away, his basketball shorts framing his ass perfectly.

"I feel like I need to take my shirt off now just so you'll look at me like that," says Jesse with a laugh, leading me into the school.

"Like what?" I ask.

"Like you want to eat me."

I blush and try to scurry away, but he holds onto me. "Did you forget we have our first class together?" he asks innocently.

"I was under the impression that History class is optional for you," I tell him with a sugary smile. It seems to catch him off guard because he stops walking and just kind of looks at me with a dazed expression. He shakes his head a little and starts to walk again, pulling me forward since his arm is still latched around my shoulders.

"Someone has recently appeared that has suddenly made History the most fascinating class I've ever attended."

I roll my eyes but can't help but feel flattered. I can feel how shocked the rest of the students are when he strolls in with me. Although I was only joking about the fact that History was optional for him, by the looks on our classmates' faces, I wasn't far off the mark.

"Oh my gosh, oh my gosh, oh my gosh," mouths Amberlie to me when I take a seat next to her, and Jesse takes a seat behind me and immediately starts to play with my hair. She looks like she's about to have a full-on panic attack about the fact that Jesse just walked into the room with me. "You have to tell me everything," she mouths, and I can't help but laugh at her exuberance.

Jesse surprises me by actually making some very smart comments in class and I wonder what else he hides behind the sunny mask he wears. He walks me to my next class, not giving Amberlie a chance to accost me in the hallway. I'm disappointed that I don't see Tanner and Jensen, and then I'm immediately disappointed in myself for even having that thought.

"Tell me everything," squeals Amberlie from beside me. I've been so lost daydreaming about the guys that I forgot that I had this class with her.

"What do you mean?"

"Twenty people said they saw you get out of Jesse Carroway's truck this morning," she said, her eyes going dreamy for a second as if she's imagining it was her who rode in the truck.

"You talked to twenty people about this?" I ask quizzically.

"That's not the point. Just talk," she squeals.

"I walk to school and he was just being nice," I tell her with a shrug, picking up my pencil to start taking notes when the teacher walks in.

"This isn't over," Amberlie mouths, and I shoot her a grin to let her know that I'm fully aware that I'm torturing her.

I escape out of the room before she can accost me, and I manage to not see anyone until lunchtime when I once again find myself walking into the bustling lunchroom. The difference today being that while yesterday I just felt like everyone was talking about me, today I know that they are talking about me.

Like yesterday, I get into the lunch line and make my way to the register after grabbing a sandwich and soup combo that doesn't look too gross. And just like yesterday, right as I'm about to give the lady my number for my free lunch, a hand sweeps in. This time placing a Sunkist and a Reese's on my tray.

The golden skin gives the hand away today though and I look up to see that it's Jensen paying today. I say nothing until we are out of the line and walking towards their table.

My face heats up thinking about the fact that they've automatically decided that I was too poor to be able to afford food. Which is true but isn't the point. "You don't have to do that," I say quietly, my voice trembling a lot more than I would like.

"Do what?" he asks in a gruff voice.

"Pay for my lunch. I... I get it for free," I say so softly that I'm not quite sure he can even hear me.

"Baby, we're going to pay for your lunch every day because we like you and that's just what we decided. We're rich as fuck and we're only going to be richer when we make it big. It's not a big deal."

I didn't know what he meant by "make it big." As far as I knew none of them were athletes, although seeing Jensen's body this morning, he sure looked like one. My mouth salivates a bit just thinking about it.

Instead of asking Jensen what the heck he's talking about I decide to ask Amberlie so I don't come across as so ignorant.

Jensen leads me to their table where this time there's an open seat in between Jesse and Tanner. Jesse gives me a sexy wink as I sit down, and I can't help but blush. Tanner reaches across and grabs the Sunkist and the Reese's from my tray, ripping open the package and putting one of the treats on my tray after he takes the other one for himself. It's only the second day that I'm eating with them and yet this feels like a routine, something that we've been doing forever, that we will do forever. I've never had something like that before.

Tanner and I are debating the correct way to eat a Reese's when a throat clears from behind us. I look up in time to see the gorgeous blonde from the other night sitting down in Tanner's lap. She looks comfortable there, like she belongs. I hate it.

"Reagan, what are you doing?" he asks wearily.

"Did something change between a few days ago and now?" she asks, a nervous look on her face as she fidgets in his lap.

"I believe you have a seat somewhere down there," drawls Jesse, motioning towards the end of the table where the other two girls from the other night are sitting at the end of the table, beautiful scowls on both of their faces.

She leans in to try and whisper something to Tanner but evidently, he's had enough as he practically pushes her off his lap. The girl is close to tears and she looks at him for a moment beseechingly before she turns and snarls at me. "Make sure to have fun while it lasts, little girl. You won't hold his attention for long," she says to me.

Suddenly the situation is too much. I've spent my entire life laying low and all of the attention from the guys, from the other students...it's too much for me. I can feel the start of a panic attack coming on, so I stand up quickly, aware that it's going to look like I'm running away but unable to control myself enough to stop.

I practically sprint out of the lunchroom, hearing the faint roar of one of the guys yelling something as the doors close behind me. I barely make it to the bathroom before I'm throwing up. After there's nothing left in my stomach, I huddle in a ball in the corner. I know that it's disgusting that I'm sitting on the floor of a public bathroom, but I feel so shaky and out of sorts that I can't do anything about it. I hear the door of the bathroom open and someone walks in. I try to quiet my sobs, so I won't attract any attention to myself. I look up realizing that in my haste to make it to the toilet I forgot to lock the stall.

It suddenly opens and I'm shocked to see that Jensen is standing there. Out of the three of them I would have expected him the least likely to play the role of the white knight in shining armor. He crouches down in front of me.

"What's going on, baby?" he asks. I never thought I was into endearments or pet names before, but the way he says "baby" makes me feel fluttery inside.

"I have trouble with attention," I say quietly.

"Attention?" he asks quietly.

"It's hard for me when people look at me, or even talk to me. I'm a sidelines kind of girl. Someone who's really good at blending in with the crowd. It just was too much with everyone staring," I whisper, my voice shaking as I try to explain something that I know is stupid.

Jensen strokes the side of my face gently and I find myself leaning in to it.

"You're not a sidelines girl. It would be impossible not to notice you or pick you out in any crowd. You just have never noticed before how much people watch you."

I laugh at him, thinking he must be joking but my laughter fades when I notice how serious his face stays. He tilts up my chin.

"I would love to tell you more about everything special about you, but I would rather not do it on the floor of the girls' bathroom," he says. I'm sure that I'm beet red at this point. I was so caught up in Jensen's magic that I completely forgot that I was sitting on the floor of the bathroom and had just thrown up.

He takes my hand, unfazed that it needs to be cleaned from touching the floor and leads me out of the stall. After I wash my hands, he takes my hand again and leads me out into the hallway. I was expecting the hallway to be packed, hundreds of faces lined up interestedly to see why Jensen Reid is loitering in the girls' bathroom, but the hallway is a ghost town. I look up at Jensen in surprise.

"Tanner and Jesse took care of it," he says with a shrug.

I let out a long breath. "I guess I need to head to class. It's only my second day and I'm already wishing I could skip."

"We can if you want to," he says, pulling me close. I can smell his musky scent and it's doing things to my hormones. His eyes are flicking to my mouth and I find myself fantasizing about what it would be like to touch that body that I got to see this morning. The bell rings, signaling that I'm officially late for class, and the spell is broken.

I push away and start walking backwards away from Jensen who's staring at me and looking a little out of breath. It takes everything in me to turn around and jog to class. I'm not sure what has gotten into me. I've never acted like this before.

I work extra hard to concentrate in the rest of my classes. It takes much more energy than classes at my old school and I know I'm going to be in trouble here if this keeps up. Amberlie accosts me in the hallway as I'm walking to the front of the school to walk home.

"You're going tonight, right?" she asks expectantly. I'm just now settling down from the lunchroom debacle and my interlude with Jensen, so I'm quite certain that I'm not going anywhere tonight unless I'm forced to because some kind of drunken brawl between Terry and David forces me to leave.

She's looking at me so excited though that I humor her by asking what she's talking about.

"They didn't mention it to you?" she asks confusedly. "That's weird," she whispers to herself.

"I still don't know what you're talking about," I tell her.

"I'm talking about the fact that the guys have a show tonight and everyone is going to be there!" she exclaims.

"A show?" I ask, more confused than ever.

"What have you been talking about with the guys if you don't know that they're in a band...the most amazing band in the world? It's only a matter of time before they make it big," she gushes. She looks at me suddenly, somehow even more excited than she was a second ago. "You've been making out with them, haven't you?" she squeals. "Why would you guys be talking when you could be sticking your tongue down their throats. Oh my gosh, you have to tell me everything. How did they taste? Did they cop a feel?"

"Amberlie!" I say rather loudly, garnering stares.

"What?" she asks.

"We haven't kissed. Their band just didn't come up. If I can remind you, I've only been here for two days."

She looks really disappointed at my announcement, but it doesn't keep her down for long. "Well, you still have to come tonight. I'm sure they're expecting you to be there. I'm so excited for you to hear them for the first time. It's a freaking religious experience," she says so excitedly that I expect her to throw out some "Hallelujahs" at any minute.

Despite what I said to her, in the back of my mind I'm wondering why they didn't say anything about tonight. Maybe they didn't want me to go. Maybe I shouldn't go.

"Stop looking like your puppy just got kicked," she says, yanking me with her towards where her red Volkswagen sits jauntily in the parking lot. "Let's stop by your house to get your stuff and then we can get ready at my house," she says.

"No," I say loudly, stopping in my tracks. There's no way I'm showing her where I live. With my luck Terry and David would be cooking meth or having an orgy on the one day that I brought a friend over. While Amberlie isn't driving a sports car that looks like a spaceship, it's obvious she has money since her car is brand new. She would probably never speak to me again if she saw how I lived.

Amberlie looks a little hurt at my stern tone so I hurry to smooth it over with her. "My house is a mess and I don't really have anything to wear anyway. Let's just go to your house to get ready," I tell her pleadingly.

She accepts my excuse and soon we're on our way to the side of town that's a far cry from my trailer park. We pull into the driveway and walk into her house and I shit you not, her mother is waiting in the kitchen with fresh baked cookies and milk. I feel like I've entered an episode of "Leave it to Beaver" and while it seems so wholesome that it can't be real, I'm fiercely jealous of Amberlie's life in that moment. I can't even imagine what it would be like if Terry ever had cookies waiting for me when I came home from school or was excited to see me. Hell, at this point I would be thrilled if she just had food in the house for me to eat. I'm quiet as I watch Amberlie and her mother interact with each other. Mrs. Hastings is kind and welcoming and fits the part perfectly of everything a mother should be. It's hard for me to follow Amberlie upstairs when she decides that it's time for us to get ready because I want to hang out with her mom more.

"Your mother is awesome," I tell her quietly as she rifles through her closet looking for something that will fit me. I'm at least three inches taller than Amberlie and she packs a lot more curves than I do, but Amberlie is convinced that there is something that will work.

"Yes, she is," says Amberlie absentmindedly as she throws a leather skirt at me.

I wrinkle my nose at it. I can already tell that it's going to show a lot more skin than I'm used to. "Just try it on," she says, throwing a sleeveless black top at me.

"Isn't this a bit dressed up for a concert?" I ask as I start to slip into the skirt.

"Honestly it's not dressed up enough," she says, her voice muffled as she starts to look for what she's going to wear. "But since you're hotter than sin and already have the guys salivating over you even with what you wear to school, it should be enough."

"What's wrong with what I wear to school?" I ask, amused. I'm fully aware that my thrift store finds leave a lot to be desired. Amberlie pulls her head out, her face chagrined as she starts to apologize for the slight.

"No, it's fine," I tell her with a laugh. "I don't have a lot of money for clothes," I say more somberly. Her eyes soften as she looks at me.

"Forget I said anything. You're lucky to look gorgeous in anything," she says, and I can tell that she means it. In that moment I realize that I might have made my first real friend.

After we've spent more time getting ready than I have probably in my whole life combined, Amberlie deems us ready to go. She's wearing a skin-tight emerald dress that has a snake skin design on it with over the knee high heeled black boots. It looks far more suited to a fancy night club than a local concert, but what do I know? She's so amped for the concert though that I'm getting nervous, wondering if there's going to be a million people there and if I'm going to be able to handle it.

I manage to make it into Amberlie's car without running away, and we set off. The concert is being held in a converted warehouse on the outskirts of town. As we drive into the gravel parking lot, I'm shocked at how many cars there are already even though the show doesn't start for another thirty minutes. There's a line snaked around almost the entire building.

"There's no way we're going to get in," I tell her, fully prepared to get back into the car and leave.

"No way, girly," she says. "No backing out now. There's always a list, and I have a sneaking suspicion that you're going to be on it."

I scoff at her but follow behind, a tenuous hope building inside of me that the guys had just assumed I had heard about the show and were planning on me coming. We walk up to the entrance where an enormous bald man with more muscles than I've ever seen is holding a clipboard.

"Name," he says in a bored tone.

"Ariana Kent plus one," Amberlie replies. He finds my name immediately and Amberlie turns towards me and mouths "Oh my gosh," before turning back towards the bouncer who is signaling us in. I keep my eyes averted from the crowd in line since I can hear a lot of groans and obscenities coming from it. I don't blame them. I have no idea why the guys thought enough of me to put me on a list when they obviously have their pick of admirers.

Having my name on the list gives me a funny feeling inside, one I'm not accustomed to. I try not to examine it too closely. I've learned to keep my expectations low in life. It helps keep the inevitable disappointment at a minimum.

We walk in to the warehouse and it's already so packed that I'm not even sure if we'll be able to stay in it. Amberlie takes control though, grabbing my hand and beginning to force her way to the front. As we push through the crowd, I see Reagan and the other two girls from that first night already there with beers in their hands. I guess they must have fake I.D.s or this place doesn't check. They're dressed to impress, wearing similar outfits from when I first saw them, meaning that there's more skin than fabric. They are wearing mile high heels and they look good. I feel even more underdressed seeing them. They shoot me a look when they see me, and Reagan gives me a smug smile with a little finger wave that has me wondering what she has up her sleeve.

Amberlie keeps pulling me forward. The air is heavy with sweat and anticipation so thick that I can almost taste it. Amberlie was trying to describe their sound to me in the car, but she didn't do a very good job of it. She basically said that they were a mix of "everything good about music", which wasn't very helpful. She somehow manages to pull us almost all the way to the front and even manages to convince two guys to let us share their table. The guy next to me has jet black hair with streaks of green in it that almost match his almost too vibrant eyes. Before meeting the guys, I probably would have thought that he was really attractive, but he isn't doing anything for me in comparison to them right now. I'm obviously doing a lot for him though. After telling me his name is Danny, he proceeds to stare at me and pepper me with awkward questions that I have no intention of answering.

I'm grateful when the lights darken, and smoke starts to spit out on the stage. The crowd quiets down and then all of a sudden starts to freak out so loudly that I have to cover my ears for fear that I'm going to go deaf. I get the urge to start screaming too though when the guys begin to step out on the stage. Jesse comes out first and sits behind the drums. He looks cockier than ever with his black skinny jeans and a white tank that show off how ripped he is. His blonde hair looks silver in the lighting and I'm practically salivating with how good he looks. Jensen comes out next. He picks up a guitar and starts to tune it, ignoring the screams of the girls in front of him who are begging for his attention. I see a pair of panties hit him in the face and he gives a little grin which makes the girls get even louder. He's dressed in a pair of tight jeans that showcase his ass perfectly and his hair is all over the place. He looks like he just had sex, which could be the case based on the attention he's getting. Tanner's last to step out on the stage even though Amberlie explained to me that they all take turns singing different songs so there's no real lead singer. When he steps out to the mic, I swear I see at least ten girls look like they are hyperventilating, a few are even crying.

Tanner is dressed in all black, including a pair of black

leather pants that I'm sure is going to act as a sweatbox during the show. The effect is so worth it though. I'm staring so intensely at the guys that when Tanner's silver eyes lock on my face, it catches me so off guard that I lose the ability to breathe. His beautiful eyes, hinting at some unspoken complexity, are only the tip of the iceberg of what makes him attractive, and I can't help but admire the whole package. His eyes flick to where Danny is still trying to get my attention and a flash of irritation sounds on his face. He walks to the side of the stage for a second and says something to one of the security guys. I'm shocked as the security guy then walks to my table and mutters something in Danny's ear. When Danny starts to argue, the security guy grabs him roughly by the arm and starts to drag him away.

Amberlie smirks at me. "Someone was jealous," she says, nodding her head in the direction of the guys who are still tuning their instruments.

I venture a look at the stage and see Tanner looking at me, like he was waiting for me to pay him attention. He gives me a small grin that belies the look of possession that I see in his eyes. That squirmy feeling that I've had since my name was on the list begins to grow.

Instruments finally ready, a grunge-sounding guitar rips into a few chords and sends the already crazy crowd into hysteria. I've never seen anything like this for a local band. People are acting like we're watching Nirvana or Imagine Dragons play.

The melody starts, and it's hard and fast. Tanner's voice remains low and steady as he starts to sing about starting over and finding his way in a changed world. His voice is a thing of beauty, the perfect combination of gruff and smooth. I've never heard anything like it. I melt as I listen to the lyrics. Amberlie had told me that they write all their own stuff and I wonder how three rich kids have managed to write a song that may as well have been written for me.

Jensen steps up to the mic during the chorus, his eyes warm as if seducing a lover. He finishes his line and then tilts his head back, pushing his Adam's apple against his long neck as he breaks into a guitar solo. With the warming glow rising in my belly, a low hum falls from my lips. He's sexy as hell and I'm stunned at how they're bringing out all kinds of feelings I haven't felt since… ever.

The song ends and Jesse and Tanner switch places, Jesse grabs a guitar that someone off stage hands to him. A merciless smile presses to his lips as his fingers begin to strum a beautiful, light tune in a melody that's again so unique that I've never heard anything like it before. The music makes me ache and I'm begging for release from its torment when finally, his lips open, releasing a deliciously low note, reminiscent of the way he growled my name when he had me against the lockers the other day at school. My head's floating in the clouds as he sings about soul mates and second chances and never wanting to let go. It's beautiful and slow, overflowing with emotion. The song's almost as enchanting as the man standing in front of me, singing from his heart. Chills erupt beneath my skin, dancing up and down my spine. By the time he's done singing, my eyes are stinging with tears.

These guys are the real thing and so far out of my league.

Gentry has been strange all morning as he gets ready to leave. He's nursing quite the hangover, so I've tried to tell myself that the strangeness is because of that. I hurried getting him ready this morning in my eagerness for him to leave, and I'm worried that he's taken it as a sign that I'm hiding something. He's shot me furtive glances all morning like he's looking for my secrets.

"What are your plans for the weekend?" he suddenly asks. I frown and carefully finish folding one of his shirts before answering.

"Just the usual home stuff. I might go grocery shopping and get my nails done," I tell him, pretending to be really interested in the pair of pants that I was fake inspecting for lint. It's an unusual question since Gentry knows that I know very well that I'm not allowed to go anywhere besides those two places. I could probably get away with going to church as well as long as I sat with his parents, but other trips he's gone on I haven't even risked that. His question only serves to make

There's a heavy silence in the room while I finish folding his last piece of clothing.

"I'm going to run to the store and grab something I need for my trip," he says vaguely after I've just finished zipping up his suitcase. I look at him quizzically.

"We packed everything on your list. What are we missing?" I ask, feeling confused.

"Just a converter for my phone, and don't question me," he snaps, confusing me even more. I know better than to ask him further questions, but I have a feeling of unease as he leaves for the store and returns thirty minutes later with a bag from one of the local electronics stores.

"Can you go make me a lunch to take with me?" he asks me as he stands in the doorway of our bedroom, fiddling with the bag.

"Of course," I say quietly, walking by him and back down the stairs to the kitchen. I can feel his eyes following me down the stairs and it gives me prickles all along the back of my neck. Gentry always loves to eat out on the company's dime when he leaves on business trips. I have no idea why he would want to take a sandwich with him. I hear him come down the stairs and step outside for a moment. A few minutes pass and then he comes in just as I'm finishing up packing his lunch.

"I've got to run," he says, brushing a kiss across my cheek. He fingers my neck before grabbing it suddenly so tightly that I can feel the edges of my vision start to go black.

"You haven't forgotten who you belong to, right?" he asks, tightening his hand even more. If this isn't the day that he's chosen to finally kill me, I'm definitely going to have another bruise to add to the menagerie already covering my body.

"You," I choke out, the words feeling like acid in my throat. He stares at me for a minute more, a strange expression in his eyes as he runs them over my face as if he's trying to see inside of me. I can feel my face starting to turn blue and my body slackening as I prepare to faint.

"Be a good girl this weekend," he says before letting me go and turning abruptly to walk towards the garage. I fall to the floor, gasping for breath. He grabs his suitcase and walks through the garage door without a second look, closing it softly behind him. A few minutes later I hear the car back out of the garage and leave the cul de sac.

I let out a sigh of relief despite the fact that it feels like he just got done trying to rip my head off. It takes me another hour before I can get off the floor. I lay there soaking in the silence of the house, half-heartedly listening to make sure he doesn't come back. When I finally manage to make it to my feet, I slowly move forward with my plan. In the back of my mind, I'm worried about how I'm going to find a quiet place to talk to Gentry if he calls tonight, but I decide to deal with that later. I'll take an extra beating for not answering the phone in exchange for seeing them.

I unsteadily walk up the stairs, still unable to get rid of the lightheadedness, and struggle to pull out the suitcase under the guest bed. I had hid it there in the beginning of our marriage knowing that Gentry would never deign to look under there. Opening the suitcase, I gently touch the piles of clothes from a life I've forced myself not to think about. I pick up Amberlie's black leather mini skirt that she never would take back, the one that I had worn the first time I saw the guys play, and I let myself go down memory lane for a second. I used to love to wear it with Jesse's flannel shirts and the guys loved how it made my legs look. I hold it up in front of myself in the mirror on the wall.

When we first got married and I was still somewhat idealistic about what my life was going to be like with Gentry, I had packed all of my clothes up from the apartment that Gentry had been helping me pay for while we were dating, and moved all of my belongings into our new home in anticipation of our marriage. Little did I know that Gentry and his mother had a whole new wardrobe picked out for me. Evidently what I used to wear wasn't up to the image they wanted to portray. Looking back, replacing my clothes with what they wanted me to wear, instead of what I wanted to wear, was one of the first ways that they began to shape me into who they wanted me to be. It all escalated after that until the person staring in the mirror isn't anyone that I recognize.

"Be brave," I whisper to my reflection, tasting the words on my tongue for the first time since before everything went to hell. I've been surviving ever since I realized I couldn't escape Gentry. This was my first time in a while doing something other than just trying to survive. If I was being honest with myself though, going to this concert was me still trying to survive because as soon as I heard that they would actually be nearby I knew that if I didn't try to see them, the last remaining piece of me would break.

I slowly slip off the paisley Lily Pulitzer dress I had been wearing to send Gentry off, and I put on the skirt. It's looser than before since I barely eat nowadays. Stroking the leather, I already feel braver, more myself. I find myself wishing that I had one of Jesse's shirts. I'm sure that would go over well though. I can just see the looks on their faces if they saw me wearing that. There would be pity and disgust in their eyes as they looked at the girl that they had forgotten about but who obviously was obsessed with them just like all of their crazy stalkers.

Disgusted with the thought, I turn back towards the suitcase filled with my old clothes and continue rifling through them. Everything seems juvenile looking at it from the lens of a woman rather than a girl. I need to make something work though since Gentry has alerts on my credit cards that tell him everything I spend. There's no way for me to get cash out of the bank without him being alerted either, so I'm stuck. I'm just lucky that yesterday was my usual gas day so I didn't have to spark his interest by getting gas this weekend because of the extra distance I'm going to drive going to the concert. As it is, I'm going to have to find some quarters somewhere around the house and take the bus next week to pick up the dry cleaning and my other errands, so he doesn't get suspicious about extra miles on the car.

Frustrated, I'm just about to give up when a flash of red peeks out from the bottom of my suitcase. Grabbing it, I pull it out and feel my heart breaking a little. It's a red, long-sleeved top that's meant to hug your every curve. It has a choker neckline with a cutout around the chest and I remember when I saw it in the store, I had to have it. I had bought it to bring with me to L.A. I was going to show up in my sexy red top and get their attention, show them that I wasn't a little girl anymore. That I was theirs. I obviously never got to wear it, and it seems fitting that the first time it is worn would be to see them.

I take my time getting ready, actually enjoying the process for once. I curl my long, dark brown hair into perfect waves and then line my unusual golden colored eyes carefully with black eyeliner to make them pop. I'm someone else tonight. Not the prisoner of an abusive man, but a twenty-three-year-old woman with a fantastic night at her fingertips. My hair and the choker neckline hides the burgeoning bruises on my neck perfectly. I finish off my costume by painting my lips a dark crimson color that Gentry never lets me wear because he says that I look like a prostitute. The red makes me feel powerful and judging by the fact that I feel like I'm going to puke my guts out the closer I get to the time of the concert, I need all the empowerment I can get. I tuck the lipstick and some powder into a small black purse that I throw over my shoulder, and then I grab my keys. Right before I leave, I pause, remembering the last time I saw them.

"Four months, Princess. If you're not at that airport in four months, I'll come here and drag you back to us myself. Understand?" Tanner asks, brushing a kiss across first my forehead, then my cheeks, and finally my lips. I can feel the eyes of the guys on us. As time has passed, they've become increasingly affectionate in front of each other, but it still feels strange to me. Tanner takes a step back, making room for Jensen to take his place.

"Baby," he whispers in my ear. His hands thread through my hair. He sounds almost like he's trying not to cry. I'm already there, tears are streaming down my face and soaking his t-shirt that I've buried my face in. "Just promise..." he says, leaving the rest unspoken. There's not a situation that I can imagine that would prevent me from joining them. I tell him that, making promises that I'd wager my life on that I will keep. He takes a step away from me and then stalks out of the room, not looking back.

Jesse steps up last. He wraps his whole body around me, and I try to memorize what it feels like to be this warm, to feel this loved. "Pretty girl," he sighs, pulling back and rubbing his chest with a distraught look on his face. "I'm not sure how I'm going to make it until you join us."

I've never seen Jesse look so pained and I want to throw all my plans to the wind and just go with them right now. The only thing that stops me is that I have to be able to bring something to the table with me when I join them. Even if it's just a high school diploma now, I'll take college classes when I'm on the road with them in graphic design or something. I'll do whatever it takes to be an asset to them rather than a hindrance. It's the only way that this strange relationship of ours will work once they make it big.

"Take my heart with you and keep it safe," I tell him, knowing that it sounds corny but meaning it with all the depth of my soul.

"Always," he whispers. I tilt my head up and press my lips against his, desperate for one last piece of perfection before they leave. He groans, burying his fingers into my hair and taking over the kiss. He devours my mouth with all the anxiety, frustration, and anger we are both feeling about this forced parting. When I pull back, I feel faint and I struggle to breathe. I can see Tanner's silver eyes staring at me over Jesse's shoulder, longing and lust battling inside of their depths. "Soon," he mouths, and I feel a wave of anticipation even as I give Jesse one more desperate hug and say goodbye.

Brushing a tear from my face, and thanking myself for using waterproof mascara, I walk out to my car and then start driving to my one night away from reality.

6

THEN

Seeing them perform really is a religious experience, one that I never want to give up. Like every person in this room I would love to bow at the altar of the Sounds of Us for as long as they let me. Just the thought makes me feel pathetic.

When the last note fades, I'm somewhat afraid that the whole building is going to come down since it's so freaking loud in here. I find myself screaming along with the crowd, unable to stop myself.

I choke down a glass of water that Amberlie had set down in front of me. The guy whose friend had been dragged away had wisely kept his sights on Amberlie instead of trying for me, supplying her with drinks for the entire show. She was definitely on the drunk side of tipsy, telling me how beautiful I was and how she was so glad that we were going to be best friends in that way that girls sometimes acted when they were drunk. I had been tempted to sip some of her drink during the show since the guys couldn't seem to keep their eyes off of me and it was making me nervous, but I held off. I knew logically that there were millions of people who were able to drink alcohol with no problems at all. However, watching Terry and David destroy their lives and sometimes mine because of it made me afraid to go there. Tonight wasn't going to be the night I tried it no matter how badly I wanted to.

The guys are all in the front of the stage, huge smiles on their faces as they slap hands with their out of control fans. I knew in that moment that someday I would be seeing them perform on a stage with a hundred thousand fans instead of the two hundred or so that are packed into the room. Besides the talent they obviously possess in spades, there is some intangible quality about them that told you they were special. That they were better than everyone else. In that moment I knew it was inevitable that they would leave, and I found myself already missing them.

Tanner jumps off the stage and starts to wade his way through the crowd, never taking his eyes off of me despite the girls who pull at him for attention as he passes. Amberlie had started making out with her guy or I'm sure she would have been drooling about how unbelievably hot Tanner looks right now. At some point in the show he had ripped off his shirt and there is a light sheen of sweat all over his chest highlighting a body that's as sinful as Jensen's was this morning. Seriously, are these guys even real human beings? I had seen David with his shirt off and there was nothing there but a beer gut and an unruly patch of hair in awkward places all over his chest. Tanner's body looks nothing like that. My fingers itch to trace the hard ridges on his abdomen; he's beautifully sculpted everywhere. Undeniably masculine, and dripping sex appeal, intricate tattoos started on the left side of his chest, wrapping around his shoulder before covering his entire left arm, raising an air of mystery and danger around him. Looking closer I can see a few faded scars marking his body. If anything, they add to the sex appeal that is Tanner.

I watch him until he's standing right in front of me and even then, I forget how to speak when he first asks me if I liked the show since I'm so busy gaping at his gorgeousness.

"Well?" he asks, and I realize that it's probably been at least a minute since he first asked his question.

"You were amazing," I tell him hoarsely, choking up since there's no good way for me to describe what I just witnessed. His eyes soften as he looks at me and I know he can tell what I'm trying to say.

"I think we went all out for you tonight, Princess. I don't think we're usually that good."

I blush, wondering how many other girls he's said the same thing to. "You didn't tell me about tonight," I blurt out suddenly, needing to know why before I went any farther down the path I knew tonight was leading me.

He looks confused for a second and then he takes my hand in his, pulling me off my chair and into his body so we're lined up perfectly. It's a little bit sickening how even his sweat smells good. I have to force myself not to lean in further so I can take a big whiff. My nerves are on overdrive being this close to him. A thought flickers in my mind of what it felt like for Jensen to be on the other side of me yesterday. I push it away quickly.

"Princess, we didn't think you would be up to coming after what happened today. Jensen told us how much anxiety you had, and we didn't want to pressure you into anything that would make it worse." He gestures to the packed, raucous room around us. "We didn't know if you would be able to handle all of this."

He leans in close and it feels like my heart is about to beat out of my chest. "Seeing you in the crowd was the best surprise that I could have asked for though," he says, his voice fading into a whisper as his lips inch closer to mine.

I've just closed my eyes and am awaiting the kiss that I know is coming when someone bumps the side of Tanner and almost sends me flying.

"What the fuck?" he says, catching me before I hit the ground. We both look over and see that Reagan is there. Her boobs are pushed up so high at the moment that they are almost at her chin. She looks incredibly mature and sexy, and I suddenly want to leave.

"Can I talk to you for a minute?" she says with a wide, fake smile. Tanner sighs, raking a hand through his still sweaty hair.

"What do you need, Reagan?" he asks.

I take a step away, but his arm tightens around me preventing me from going anywhere. His fingers begin to strum up and down the side of my ribs. Reagan's eyes dart to his hand and they tighten with rage and frustration before she forces herself to look friendly and easy-going once again.

"I just wanted to tell you about what Daddy said about the band," she says. Tanner stiffens and I can tell he wants to know what she has to say.

"Reagan's father is a record producer in Atlanta," he explains to me, and I like him even more in that moment for making me feel like I'm a part of the conversation.

"Let's talk about it at the party with the other guys," he says charmingly. The smile he flashes her is big, but I realize that it's fake. He gave me a real smile the other day and I haven't forgotten what that looked like.

"You promise we can talk then?" Reagan asks, her voice coming out a bit pleading at the end. I feel sorry for her in that moment. She's using every tool at her disposal, even industry contacts, to try and keep Tanner interested, and I know that it's not going to work.

After Tanner nods she prances back to her friends, her steps lighter with the hope of a successful night. I push any thoughts of her out of my mind when Tanner once again envelops me in both arms.

"You're going to come to the after-party, right?" he asks, a hint of vulnerability in his question as if there was any way that I would say no to getting the chance to hang out with them more.

I look back at Amberlie who looks like she's about to eat the face of the guy she's making out with. "I want to, but I might need a ride," I say with a laugh. He looks behind me and winces. "You're definitely coming with us," he says, taking my hand and beginning to lead me back towards where Jesse and Jensen are now signing various items of clothing that are being thrown at them by still-screaming girls.

I stop him. "I need to make sure someone gives her a ride home, she's been drinking," I explain, and his gaze once again softens as he looks at me. "Princess, you're too sweet to be true," he says.

"You've been hanging out with the wrong people if you haven't seen them arrange rides for their friends," I say with a laugh.

I walk back to the table and grab Amberlie's phone to use her Uber app. I don't have any special data on my phone that allows for apps since my phone is a free one that David and Terry got from the government. When I saw it in the mail, I swiped it before they could get their hands on it and try to sell it. It didn't have any special features, but it was nice having some sort of lifeline when I did need to make a call.

After explaining to Amberlie that an Uber is coming I still feel hesitant to leave her drunk with this guy.

"Brad is a good guy," says Tanner, doing that what's up head nod with the guy in question as he says that. "He won't try anything if she's too drunk."

Trusting Tanner to know these people way better than I do, I tell Amberlie to call me if she needs anything and I allow him to finally drag me through the crowd. We get up by the stage and immediately Jesse and Jensen's eyes are locked on me.

"Let's go," says Tanner and they jump down to join us. Jesse seems more amped up than any of them and he picks me up suddenly and swings me around.

"Alright, pretty girl. It's time for you to tell me how amazing I am," he says with a smile and I can't help but giggle as he sets me down again.

"You were okay," I tell him with a wink, and he fake pouts.

"I bet you told Tanner he was amazing tonight, didn't you? It's because he took his shirt off. And Jensen took his shirt off this morning. So, you probably think he was amazing tonight as well. Nope, this isn't happening. Prepare yourself. It's going to get hot," he says with a sexy wink, letting me go and ripping his tank top down the middle in a way that elicits screams from the girls hovering around us.

My jaw drops. It has indeed gotten hot.

Just like my reaction after I saw Jensen and Tanner's bodies, I never would've believed guys with this type of a body existed in real life if I wasn't seeing them with my own eyes. I went on one date with a football player at my old school, but he wasn't built anything like this. The words "bella vie" are penned in swirling cursive across his broad chest and the word "trust" rests over his heart. I forget how to breathe when I see that both of Jesse's hardened nipples are pierced. It's so unexpected that out of the three of them, he's the one with pierced nipples. I'm at a total loss for words. He's perfection, they all are. Strong bodies, so far charming personalities, insanely talented voices, and the most beautiful freaking eyes that I've ever seen...

"Holy shit," I manage to squeak, slowly running the pad of

my thumb across the ink on his heart. I draw my eyes back up to look into his beautiful eyes and feel another earth-shattering shiver strike my core. "You're unreal."

Jesse smirks and I know I've given him the reaction he was looking for. He unexpectedly picks me up and tosses me over his shoulder as he starts to stalk backstage. "We're keeping her," he yells out to the guys as they follow behind us. I can't help but smack Jesse's butt as he walks since it's right in front of me, but he doesn't let me down until we're safely ensconced backstage, the roar of their fans fading as soon as the door closes.

We're all alone in the room and it's almost more than I can take being in there with just the three of them. Jesse sets me down and saunters away to grab a bottle of water from a table that's also filled with a bunch of random snacks. He tosses me one of the other bottles before going to grab a new shirt from a bag sitting on the faded, green couch in the room. Jesse and Tanner banter back and forth about the show as they grab their things.

Jensen slides up next to me. "Want to ride with me to the party?" he asks in that gravely voice of his that makes my knees weak.

I nod and he flashes me a beautiful grin. I savor it, because I can already tell Jensen doesn't give his smiles out lightly and I've been lucky enough to get a couple since we've met.

He takes my hand, pulling me behind him as he leads me to the back exit. "We'll meet you guys there," he says in a voice that doesn't leave any room to question him.

"I call next time," Jesse yells from behind us.

I look over my shoulder and blow him a kiss, surprising myself and them with my attempt at flirting. Feeling like a fool I turn quickly back around, Tanner's quiet laughter following me out the door.

Jensen leads me to a black Escalade. As we walk, he pulls a phone out of his pocket and types something briefly before returning the phone to his pocket. "We can stop and get food on the way to the party," he says. I try to think if I have any money with me. Pretty sure I don't. I'll just have to order a water and pretend like I've already eaten.

He opens the door for me, and I hesitate for a second looking into the luxurious interior. I look back at him patiently waiting. Under the streetlights, his beauty feels dangerous, like it could lure me in and never let me go. I get inside.

We drive for a while in silence. When we get to a red light, Jensen turns and stares at me. "Just to make it perfectly clear that I'm interested in you, I'll ask the standard first date question... as lame as it is. Tell me more about yourself," he says with a smirk.

I brush my hair behind one ear and look down at the floor. Did he really just say first date? Are we on a date? The idea that he could actually want to date me freezes my brain per usual and I end up giving my standard lame answer. "I'm nothing special," I say bitterly.

"Ari," he barks at me suddenly, making me jump in my seat. "I don't want to hear you talk that way about yourself again. Are we clear?" he asks.

I stare back at him wide-eyed. "Okay," I softly whisper. He leans back in his seat and turns his gaze back to the road as the light turns green. I look at him out of the corner of my eyes.

"I don't like to talk about myself," I begin to explain, wanting him to understand the darkness and insecurity that lay within me, but not knowing how to put it into words. "Just give me time to get there."

He nods and puts his hand on my leg, stroking the skin beneath my skirt softly with his thumb.

"I like this skirt on you," he says, his hand inching up

slightly and sending shivers down my spine. I'm frozen in place as he finally moves his hand and grabs mine. It's the first time I've held hands with a guy. Having a mother who likes to spread her legs has made me quite timid about anything that could potentially lead me in her footsteps. Pushing my fears aside, I savor how my hand feels in his.

"I used to want to sing," I randomly tell him, feeling immediately stupid since any talent I have pales considerably to theirs.

"Huh…" He frowns the tiniest bit.

"What?"

"I've just had a lot of girls tell me that they want to be singers," he says with a laugh, sounding a bit disillusioned at the thought.

I'm annoyed with myself for saying anything. Of course he's going to think that I'm just trying to ride his coattails or something. But then again, why the hell do I care what this almost stranger thinks about my life's dream? I don't know why… but for some reason, I did.

"I'm sorry," he says sheepishly. "I'm passing judgment without even hearing you sing."

I shrug. "You probably won't ever hear me sing. It's just a pipe dream, forget I said anything."

He brings my hand to his lips. "I don't want to forget anything you say. I'm sorry I reacted that way. Forgive me?"

He sounds so sincere and upset that I can't help but forgive him.

"Nothing to be sorry for," I assure him, wiggling in my seat from the sensation his lips left on my hand. I look at him out of the corner of my eye for the longest time as he drives. Probably ten seconds go by before I realize I'm staring. This first date, if you can call it that, is officially entering disaster territory.

"So… how did you get into music?" I finally ask him. He

looks at me for a long moment before he answers – like he is gauging me. Like maybe he is wondering how much he should open up to me. Then he starts talking.

"The first time I ever knew what I wanted was when I was five years old and I heard Nirvana's 'Smells Like Teen Spirit' for the first time on the radio. You know that song?"

"Of course. Who doesn't?" I say with a laugh.

"I remember being hypnotized by the guitar at the beginning. The way Krist Novoselic's fingers just dance over the strings. And then Dave Grohl comes in and you're hooked. Kurt Cobain was who did it for me though. His vocals are so...different... he sings all these nonsensical words and of course the song is really about teenage freedom and revolution, but the way he sings the lyrics could mean a million different things. I obviously didn't understand any of it at the time – I mean, I was five years old, I couldn't have explained it – but that song took me on a trip. It made me feel something I'd never felt before."

I watch his face as he tells me this story. He means every single word. He is absolutely transported as he tells it… …and, I have to admit, I'm moved by how passionate he is about it. He smiles and continues.

"My dad owns a flooring business, but he's been obsessed with rock n' roll his entire life– that's where I think I get my love of music from. Anyway, he was sitting there watching me the entire time, and after it was over, he asked me if I liked it. And all I said was, 'Again!'"

I had to laugh. He said it exactly the way a five-year-old would say it – full of exuberance and innocence and impatience.

"So, my dad takes me into the back of his store where he had a guitar, and he played the song, and we both sang it together. He taught me the words, and I made him sing it over and over and over." Jensen smiles, a little ironically. "Other kids have 'Three Blind Mice'. I had 'Smells Like Teen Spirit.'"

His eyes trail off into the distance, and his voice takes on an edge of melancholy.

"It's one of the best memories I have of my father. He's an overall pretty shitty person, especially to my mom. But in my head, I feel like he loves me just because he kept playing that damn song over and over and over again. Never said 'no, let's stop'… he just kept playing it."

Jensen's voice trails off as we pull into the local pizza place. We sit there in silence for a moment and I'm just about to say something when he continues.

"But it's also a great memory because it was like I was hit by a bolt of lightning. It was the first time I ever realized that people actually do this for a living. They play guitar and sing. That's what they do. That meant I could do that, too. Not only that, but… the song just made me feel. In the space of three minutes, I went from hypnotized and happy, to in love, to feeling pain and loss, and every fucking second was beautiful. And from that moment forward, I knew what I wanted to do in life: I wanted to be a musician. I wanted to make music and sing. And I wanted to make other people feel, the way that song had made me feel. Feel everything."

He stops talking and looks at me – a little shy, a little hesitant, a little embarrassed. It's hard to explain my emotions. His words had the same effect on me that "Smells Like Teen Spirit" had on his five-year-old self. He's made me feel- totally and completely. I could see the passion and the realness in him. It was unmistakable. And after that story, I was so totally into this guy. If he leaned over right then and kissed me, there was no way I could have resisted.

He leans in and I wonder if it's going to happen, but instead he closes his eyes for a second and takes a deep breath.

"Should we go in and get some pizza?" he asks.

"Yeah," I tell him with a smile. He hops out of the car and runs over to open my door for me, making me blush for the millionth time in the night when he grabs my hand as we walk.

We go inside, I assume to grab a bunch of pizzas to go, but he surprises me when he asks the hostess for a booth. "Is it okay if we eat here?" he asks, that hint of vulnerability lingering in his question once again.

"I'd like that," I tell him, and I'm sure there are stars shining out of my eyes as we're led to our table.

The waitress comes by and it's like I don't even exist as she stares at him and directs all of her questions towards him. He nods at her when she arrives but redirects all the questions to me. "This is a make or break it moment," he says. "Does pineapple belong on pizza?"

I fake a gagging noise. "Fruit does not belong on pizza," I tell him sternly, only half joking since I have pretty strong feelings on the subject.

He fakes wiping his forehead. "Thank goodness. I don't have to leave," he says with a wink.

The waitress rolls her eyes at our exchange although I know she would trade anything to be on the receiving end of his corniness.

We decide on a meat lover's pizza and two Caesar salads. Conversation is easier over food for some reason. It feels like the bustle of the restaurant makes me not feel so much the center of attention although his eyes haven't left my face the entire time. I keep wiping my face to make sure that I don't have any pizza sauce on it.

"What are your parents like?" he asks. I still for a moment, trying to think of how to explain Terry and David. Then I think of the story that he told me, and I feel like maybe it would be okay to share something personal about myself for once.

"They're the worst," I tell him and watch as his eyes widen at my honesty. Words continue to tumble out of my mouth. "They spend most of their time either drunk or high and constantly cheat on each other, and the police are called all the time because of their fights. That's why I was out walking the other night when I saw you guys at the campfire, the police had just arrived, and I snuck out the window because I didn't want to have to deal with it all the night before I started at my new school. It's why I always have second hand clothes and I get a free lunch at school. I live in the trailers on Park Road and you drive a new Escalade at seventeen years old and have the whole world at your fingertips once you graduate, meaning that we're about as far apart as two people can be."

He's shaking his head before I finish my last sentence. "You'll find this out in time, but the three of us? We're best friends because we're all broken in different ways. You'll see it eventually. I don't want to tell you right now because I don't want you to run, but baby...you being broken means that for once we've found someone that is like us."

I stare at him, wanting to believe in the words that he's saying. It seemed impossible that these beautiful boys could be broken like me, but a small, evil part inside of me rejoices at the thought. I wouldn't have to be alone anymore.

Jensen pays for the meal after we get two more pizzas to go for Tanner and Jesse who are probably starving if they haven't eaten since before the show. Jensen balances the pizza boxes in one hand and grabs my hand with his other. After he tosses the pizzas onto the floor of the backseat, he lightly pushes me into his car and leans over me, his lips getting closer and closer. I involuntarily moan because I want this kiss so bad.

He gives me an amused look at the sound, and I want to melt into the ground from embarrassment.

The kiss that follows, the gentle exploration of my mouth. I never look away, never lose eye contact, and my heart surges. I've been so afraid of loving and losing my entire life that I wasn't aware I had already started falling for Jensen until it had already started. I feel things for Jensen. I feel happy, warm, fuzzy good things for Jensen Reid, and it's both healing and scary at the same time.

7

NOW

I pull up to the concert venue. It's in the new stadium that was built for the state's NFL team. It's a testament to modern architecture with its sleek lines and windows that extend the whole length of the building. I had always wanted to come take a tour but it was just another thing that Gentry wouldn't let me do. He had taken a tour with his work and had gone to a game last year with a client, and as he put it...why would it make sense for him to take me to do something he had already done?

The parking lot is beyond packed already considering I've come two hours before the concert actually starts. VIP guests get to show up early to meet the band, or at least that's what the radio employee had told me when he was giving me details of my prize. My mind was so shocked that I'm sure I missed some important information. I just hope that I didn't misunderstand that I could pick up the tickets or that I could actually get in early. That would be embarrassing to be barred from the venue because security thought I was trying to get to the band when I wasn't supposed to.

My palms are sweaty because I'm so nervous and I rub

them against my skirt to try and wipe them off. It makes me think of how Tanner would start rapping Eminem's Lose Yourself song anytime someone said that their palms were sweaty. "Best song ever," he would say afterwards even though everyone else would be groaning from his performance. Tanner never cared what people thought of him and it didn't matter if he did. Everyone always thought that everything he did was the coolest thing possible. He had that air around him that made people want to be him. I had always envied how he was so comfortable in his own skin. A skin that held demons under the surface for sure, but still so comfortable.

My journey down memory lane has allowed me to get to the Will Call window without losing it. A bored looking woman is sitting in the window filing her nails while she talks to the ticket person next to her. I clear my throat and her eyes fly up to see me. My hands are shaking as I explain what I'm looking for and I hand her my license for verification purposes.

"Lucky girl," she says as she finds my name on a list. She smacks her gum loudly as she reaches into a basket marked VIP and gets out a packet with my name on it. "I'd give my left nut for one of these," she tells me with a laugh. I smile weakly and take the packet with trembling hands. She notices my nervousness and gives me a knowing glance. "They might be hot as hell, but they put on pants in the morning just the same as you and me," she says kindly. I nod and thank her before walking away quickly. It would be so much easier if this was just a case of nerves because I was about to meet three superstars instead of the past loves of my life.

I look through the packet and place the backstage pass lanyard around my neck. At least one thing has gone right, and I actually had tickets waiting for me.

It takes me a few minutes to find the special backstage pass entrance and before I can get in line, my phone rings signaling that Gentry is already checking in. Looking around, I run around the corner of the building into the back of the stadium that's mostly deserted and riddled with trash and debris. I curse when I miss the call but in true Gentry style, the phone starts ringing again as he tries to call me back.

"Hi," I say, trying to slow down my breathing so I don't sound so out of breath from my sprint.

"What took you so long to answer?" he asks.

"I had set my phone down to do the laundry and didn't hear it ring until just now. I'll keep it closer to me," I tell him, hoping and praying that for once he will buy one of my lies.

"I thought you would be in the air by now," I tell him.

"It was delayed," he says sullenly, and my heart leaps out of its chest at the prospect of his flight getting cancelled and him coming back home tonight.

"How much was it delayed by?" I ask, trying to keep my voice steady so I don't sound too interested. Gentry is always on the lookout for me to be acting strangely in case I'm planning on trying to run away again so my actions and how I react to things always have to be precise.

"Just thirty minutes. I should be boarding soon," he says, and I inwardly let out a big sigh of relief.

"You're doing laundry right now?" he asks, and my heart convulses at his question. It's just another way that he's been acting strangely about this trip.

"Yep," I say, hitting a piece of scrap metal with my foot to try and make the sound of the washer door closing.

"Okay," he says distractedly. "They're calling my group number, so I have to go. But Ari…"

"Yes?" I ask, my senses tingling with dread.

"Remember what I said this morning."

I'm quiet for a moment as I listen to the reassuring sounds

of the airport coming from his phone letting me know that he is actually at the airport and not on his way to me right now. "It would be impossible for me to forget," I finally say in a voice that's nearly a whisper.

He hangs up without saying anything more and I lean against the wall, trying to calm myself down. I'm not letting Gentry ruin this for me.

Eventually I walk back around the building and I join the line of excited pass holders, mostly made up of attractive woman, waiting to be let in. The minutes pass by slowly as the line inches forward. With every step forward I take, my courage falters. What if they don't recognize me, or worse, don't remember me? Maybe I imagined how close we were. Maybe the last few years have erased me from their memory. After all, there's been a million girls in between then and now that could have replaced me and actually have contributed to a friendship or relationship with them. I was nothing but a taker.

It's finally my turn to walk through the gates. I hesitate for a moment at the entrance, wondering if I'm about to throw up. The ticket guy is leering at me and looking me up and down. His stare is enough to get me moving down the hall. His look reminds me of how Gentry looks at me and I can't get away fast enough.

I sort of remember navigating through the bustling hallways behind the stage. There's a million people around, all getting ready for the show, but their faces are a blur to me because I know, just around the corner, will be the faces that I've dreamed about for years.

As I turn the corner and see Tanner for the first time in five years, I know that I'll always remember this first sight of him. He's sitting on a faded brown leather couch, his arms extended behind him like he owns the place. In this moment he looks fitting of the titles that I've seen the media give him. He looks like he could be king of the world or the emperor of rock. He's wearing ripped jeans... a designer t-shirt that probably cost several hundred dollars and is so fitted I can see his trademark perfect abs from beneath it. He's also wearing a pair of sunglasses even though he's inside and the room itself isn't very bright. I can see the tattoos on his muscular arms even from far away. He now has full sleeves on both arms. I suddenly get the yearning to see what new tattoos are beneath his shirt. The feeling is strange because I haven't felt this sense of yearning for a man once since the day I said goodbye to all of them five years ago.

What sticks out most clearly to me however, and what I will undoubtedly remember the most, is the cocky grin he's wearing that's exactly the same as the one he would wear when I knew him. He's talking to a group of girls, all wearing the backstage passes, who are gathered around him. They are all trying to touch him, to get a piece of his brilliance. He lets out a laugh that's so familiar to me that my heart seems to actually skip a beat. I feel both jealous and happy as I bask in the sound of it. I used to be the person who made him laugh like that.

He happens to glance over, and I know when he sees me because his laugh stops abruptly. We stare at one another. "Princess?" he breathes, pushing a particularly handsy fan off of him and standing up as if he's seen a ghost. One of the girls spills her drink all over him when he pushes past her. He doesn't seem to notice. The whole room goes still as Tanner Crosby walks towards me like I'm an oasis in a desert.

This whole time I've still been hovering by the entrance of the green room, too afraid to actually enter the room. He stalks towards me until he's standing right in front of me and I feel like I'm literally about to faint. Before I can say anything, he peels off his sunglasses. I am instantly transported back five years as I stare once again into his silver eyes, still the most unique eyes that I've ever seen. His eyes are too intense and so I find myself averting my eyes down his body, to where his shirt is now plastered to his body from the spilled drink, show-casing those mouth-watering abs even more. I definitely haven't forgotten *them*. They've only gotten more defined since then.

I glance back up and I get stuck on his familiar roughly stubbled jaw. Although I avoid looking at him, I can literally feel the weight of his eyes on me. I will my mind to work. Hadn't I thought of this scenario a thousand times? Granted, it was hard to really picture what this would feel like, but hadn't I rehearsed what I would say, over and over, and pathetically, over again? But, nothing. Nothing comes to mind as he continues to stand in front of me. Time passes and I can hear people in the room start to murmur, their interest in who I am overcoming their shock that Tanner Crosby is showing interest in me at all. I still can't look up. I just stand there.

Part of me wants to look up and feast my eyes on the face I thought I would never see again in the real world. Of course, the other parts of me keep saying, don't do it. So, I just stand there dumbly as the people start to stack up behind me, desperate for their chance to come in and mingle with the band. It's funny because although I've seen Tanner in the last five years online and on the front of tabloids here and there, seeing him in person is a completely different experience.

I finally look up and our eyes clash together so intensely that I feel winded for a moment. His hair's longer, shaggier than he used to wear it. Looking closer at his chiseled face I can see that he looks … older. And bleak. And just as devas-tating to my soul as ever. As I continue to devour his face, I notice the emotions in his eyes for the first time—they're hard, angry, and breathtaking. Then he stops, his expression easing slightly.

"Ariana," he says in that sexy, low growl of his. "I've been waiting a long, long time for this."

I bolt out of the room.

I make it just around the corner before Tanner catches me. He stops me abruptly, pushing me through a doorway and then against a concrete wall as the door slams shut behind us. Reflexively, I brace myself in the momentum, feeling the abrasive cold coarseness against my heated fingertips. The intensity in his silver eyes sends a delicious shiver coursing through me. His body surrounds me, pinning me back against the wall, it's cold concrete tantalizing my overheated skin. We're surrounded by darkness.

"Leaving again?" he says in an achingly pained voice. "What was the point of making an appearance at all? Why are you here?" he whispers to me. His questions shouldn't make me feel a flash of joy, but they do. Tanner Crosby evidently has not forgotten me.

Tanner

My heart is pounding, and my breathing is choppy. Shame and humiliation pour through every fiber of my being as I stare into her eyes, at the conflicted emotions in their depths. Way. To. Go. Years spent trying to get over her and I've thrown away my pride in seven seconds. My skin flashes hot. She stares up at me with those caramel colored eyes, and I can't look away. My body lunges towards her, my arm lifting her against my chest, I'm sure crushing the air out of her. She gives a sexy gasp as she tries to get her air back and I take a moment to breathe her in, just before my mouth crashes down on hers.

My lips are hard and demanding against hers until she parts them, and I find my tongue licking into her mouth. I feel wounded, open, and … consumed. The feel of her mouth on mine is a shock of sensation. I'd only kissed her a few times all those years ago, and I've been reliving her kisses every day since the moment I'd first felt them. Even now I still crave them. I crave her. Her taste is exotic, extravagant, like something I shouldn't have. The silky slide of her tongue. She parries against me even though she can barely move with the way my hand holds her head just so. I can feel the soft press of her perfect tits against my chest and my own chest rumbles with a barely suppressed groan.

I'm madly clutching her silky hair, fisting long tufts of it, trying to hold her, to taste her. Inhaling her. When did my hands get up there? The tornado of long denied emotions and latent sexual frustration spins and tumbles and then touches down throughout my body. I'm dizzy, like we were simply sensation and emotion and had lost our bodies. Ari's arms tighten, her chest heaving, the desperation that she's leaking intoxicating me. My hands move to holding her face, my lips gentling and molding against hers. Our tongues slow and stroke, the pace becomes agonizingly sweet and infinitely more dangerous. She suddenly lets out a half-sob that slaps me in the face and I realize what the fuck I'm doing. I can't do this. With everything I have, I pull away, pull my lips from hers, struggling not to sink back into her.

She tilts her face up as I shake my head and I watch as her eyes flicker open to meet mine. Her sweet breath saws in and out, fanning across my skin. Confusion morphs into something indiscernible as her fathomless golden eyes focus on me. And then I'm cupping her face. She tries to turn her face away from me, closing her eyes, her mouth grim like she's in pain. She drops her arms that had been clenching my body.

"No," I say harshly, through gritted teeth. Pulling her in, my hands wrap around her body, gathering her close, and holding her tight against me. "Don't let go," I whisper hoarsely.

But she doesn't hold me back. My arms fall limply to my sides, and I will the beat of desire to slowly ebb from my body. It wasn't difficult now that the shame was winning out. Inhaling deeply, taking a last hit of her scent as my cheek presses against her soft hair, I steel myself to move away from her.

"Come to finish the job, then?" I ask her.

"What job?" she asks, her eyes unfocused from the severity of our kiss.

"Killing me," I growl. "Why don't you just finish the job and dig my heart out of my chest for real this time?"

I walk away, leaving her breathing heavily in the dark room behind me, the devastated look on her face tattooed into my mind.

8

THEN

I'm on cloud nine the entire car ride after Jensen's kiss as we drive to the party. We sneak looks at each other the whole time and then smile every time we catch each other. Who knew Jensen Reid could act giddy? I quickly come back to earth however when we start up a long driveway that's packed with what seems like three times as many cars as what I see in our school parking lot.

"Is this the right place?" I ask as we drive right up to the garage and pull in beside what looks like Jesse's truck. I don't look too closely to see if I'm right that it's his truck because all of my attention is focused on the biggest house that I've ever seen. It's really more like a castle than anything else, complete with what looks like turrets on either side of it. There's a large, foreboding gate that separates where we parked and the entry to the house. I can hear the rumble of a bass coming from inside the house every time people step in and out of the giant front doors that are complete with giant door knockers on them.

"This is Tanner's house," says Jensen in an amused voice at

the obvious look of wonder on my face. "His parents are never in town, so this is where we do most of our partying."

I nod like I know what he's talking about. "Where are his parents?" I ask.

Jensen's quiet for a moment before he answers. "Most likely in England where Tanner's dad's export company is based. You might have noticed the little accent Tanner has that drives the ladies crazy."

I had in fact noticed that. And it did in fact drive me crazy.

"His dad had wanted to expand the business here, so he moved the family and built this monstrosity of a house. Everything was going smoothly until his dad got caught with the live-in nanny. Tanner's mom decided they needed to go back to England, but Tanner put up a fuss. We were just starting up the band and he didn't want to leave. Tanner's parents didn't want to deal with it, so they left him here. They check in every once in a while and obviously give him money, but for the most part he's left to whatever he wants to do."

I try to think about what it would be like to be alone with a bunch of money, and I can't quite wrap my mind around it. I'm alone most of the time too, but without the money part, it hasn't been an easy experience.

Jensen distracts me from my thoughts by grabbing my hand while we walk to the door, almost like it's becoming habit.

As soon as the door to the house opens, I'm assaulted by a myriad of noises so loud that I'm already itching to run away before I take a step inside. The giant foyer right inside the door is packed with high school and college age guys and girls that are all dancing. At the top of the stairs a giant DJ booth is set up and spinning all the top hits. Jensen leads me through the room, and everyone stops to try and shake hands with him, or in all the girls' cases, to touch him and try and get his attention. He says hello to a few people but doesn't stop to talk to anyone. In the next room is a giant living room with tables set up filled with people playing beer pong and flip cup. I can see that there's a giant bar set up in the kitchen across the way where people are lined up waiting for bartenders to make their drinks.

Looking out the back windows, I see a giant pool that looks like something that would be at a resort. There's at least a hundred people out there dancing, singing, and drinking. I can see ten girls in bathing suits standing on another bar set up outside. They are dancing with each other while a crowd of guys watches and cheers. Everything is so far from any party that I've been to that my eyes bounce all around as I gape at everything. Jensen keeps walking despite the increasingly large amount of people that are trying to get his attention. He leads me up another grand staircase, down a long hallway, and opens a door...just in time for us to see Tanner snorting a line of white powder off of a table with a couple of other people. He looks up as we walk in, his face a mixture of shock and shame even as his eyes start to dilate from the drugs. Jensen mutters a low curse and I try to bolt. Drugs are something I don't do. Not after seeing how Terry and David act ...not after how touchy-feely David gets afterwards with me.

I pull away from Jensen and try to leave the room before I'm caught against a broad chest. I look up to see Jesse's gorgeous, concerned looking eyes.

"Pretty girl, don't run," he murmurs. He leads me over to where a few sectional couches are set up around a movie theatre sized screen. There's a group of extremely pretty people lounging on the couches, all looking at me interestedly, and in a lot of cases, with jealousy.

I want to look over and find Tanner, but Jesse seems hell bent on keeping me occupied. Jesse makes me sit on his lap on the couch, which firmly tells everyone around that I'm his...at least for the moment. Accepting that I'm not going anywhere for the time being, the group returns back to their conversation. It's a mix of who's hooking up with who, who was at the show tonight, whose football team is going to win tonight...it's interesting hearing the side of the pretty people for once. At my old school, I had been a loner, never really interacting with anyone besides a few dates.

Someone turns on some music and a Justin Timberlake song comes on. Jesse has both of his arms around me and he's cuddling up to me. He gets right up to my ear and then he starts singing the lyrics to me. His voice is low and rumbling and it vibrates all the way down to my toes, making the sweet spot between my legs tingle. It's no wonder why the guy's going to be a rockstar someday. Between the looks of a Greek god and the low, scratchy voice of an angel, he's extraordinary. I'm sure he has millions of women throwing themselves at his feet, desperate to feel those exquisite lips on their bodies, lips that are currently brushing against my ear and down my neck. His fingers start to slide up my leg until their inching up under my skirt like Jensen's fingers did in the car. Except Jesse shows no sign of stopping. I have enough sense about me that I'm not going to let him feel me up with twenty people watching us, so I jump off his lap and practically run to a bar that's set up in the corner, because every high school party usually has at least three fully stocked bars complete with a bartender, right?

I'm about to see if they have Diet Coke or something when I see Jensen and Tanner on the far side of the room, away from everyone else. Jensen seems to be lecturing an out of it looking Tanner. I remember the ashamed look in his eyes when I came in the room and saw him doing drugs. I wonder why he even cared what I thought. As I watch, Jensen gives him a little push and Tanner just takes it, looking down at the ground.

Jensen throws up his hands and walks out a door on the far side of the room. Tanner stands there for a second, his fists clenching and unclenching. He finally stalks over to the bar and grabs one of the full bottles of whiskey. He's just about to take a drink when I whisper his name. He freezes.

"What are you doing here, Princess?" he asks in a cold voice.

"You invited me," I say quietly. "Believe me, I wouldn't have come otherwise," I add, thinking about everything I've seen so far just walking through the house.

Tanner gets a hurt look in his eyes that's gone when I take a closer look. He takes a giant swig out of the bottle that seems to be more about making a statement to me than anything else.

"Try not to get too offended by people actually having fun," he says with a false wave of bravado. He starts to walk away.

"Tanner," I say quickly, feeling like if I let him walk away right now something bad will happen.

"What?" he says, his voice cracking a bit. I can see the tension in his shoulders as he waits to see what I'm about to say.

In that moment I see the lonely boy that Jensen didn't know he was describing. Tanner has demons...he's lost. Just like me.

"Will you watch a movie with me?" I ask, waiting nervously for his response.

He turns around and looks at me incredulously. When he sees that my face is serious, he slowly nods. I walk over to him and grab his hand, leading him to the couch where Jesse is still sitting, watching us.

"Get out," Jesse says lazily to his group of worshipers, and they all leave quickly, chagrined about being sent away.

I sit down on one side of Jesse, and Tanner sits on the other side of me after grabbing a few remotes. He dims the lights and then pulls up an app on the screen that shows a database of basically every movie that's ever been created. After some debate we decide to start The Dark Knight since we all agree that Christian Bale and Heath Ledger are magic together.

A few minutes into the movie, Tanner puts his head on my shoulder and drifts off to sleep. Jesse takes my hand in his and softly strokes it. The room must be sound proof because I can't hear any signs of the party that I'm sure is still raging all around us. In the dark room, cuddled up between two of the most gorgeous and interesting guys that I've ever met, it feels like we're in our own little world. The only thing that would make this better is if Jensen was here. It's my last thought before I drift to sleep.

When I wake up, I have no idea what time it is since the windows are all covered, and the room is dark with the exception of the soft light coming off the still on movie screen. Tanner has somehow managed to move his body so that his head is nestled in my lap with his arm wrapped around my waist. Jesse has his head on my shoulder, his hand still holding mine. I have a crick in my neck and I'm unable to say that sleeping sitting up is the way to go, but I don't dare move for fear that I will disturb them. In the soft light of the screen, Tanner looks peaceful and content. It's a very different look from the cocky face he puts on for the world. I find that I very much prefer it.

"You like to watch people when they don't know you're watching...don't you baby?" comes a quiet voice that's heavy with sleep. The appearance of the voice scares me so much that I jump in my seat. Tanner and Jesse both stir but don't wake up. Looking towards one of the other couches I see that Jensen is stretched out on one of them, a blanket thrown over him. I feel a perverse sense of pleasure that he's in the room with us instead of out with the party...or worse yet, out with another girl.

"Just push them off of you and come over here," he whispers in a gravelly voice. "They both sleep like the dead. You'll probably get to watch them mistakenly cuddle with each other at some point, which I know is probably one of your fantasies."

I roll my eyes at him even though I'm not sure he can see my face. I'm beyond exhausted and the thought of actually laying down sounds good. I try not to think about the fact that I will be lying next to Jensen.

Moving slowly, I ease out from under Tanner and Jesse's heads. Jesse's head falls back on the couch and Tanner curls up in a ball, but neither of them wake up. I grab a few blankets and put them over them before walking over to Jensen.

I get on the couch, nestling into Jensen's body in a way that appears much more familiar with him than I actually am. He's so warm and he smells so good, kind of like a spicy cinnamon, that I just want to get closer.

Jensen stills my body from its movements, and I flush, grateful for the darkness in the room, when I realize that I've woken something huge on Jensen's body. He doesn't say anything about it, just begins to stroke my hair gently. "You're going to be so good for us, baby," he says quietly.

I don't answer, but I realize that I can't remember ever feeling more protected and content than I do right now. I drift back to sleep.

"Pretty girl," Jesse's voice softly whispers as he strokes my face and brings me out of my deep sleep. I groggily open my eyes. I pat the couch behind me and realize that Jensen's gone.

Looking around I see that Tanner's gone too, and it's just Jesse and I in the room.

"Where are the others?" I ask.

"They ordered breakfast and just went downstairs to get it from the delivery guy," he says. "I won rock, paper, scissors so I got to wake you up," he says with a big, mischievous grin that makes me smile at him in return.

I get up and stretch, aware of his eyes feasting on the skin that's showing from my skirt and my shirt riding up while I slept. I don't make a move to fix them, enjoying the look in his eyes.

He groans and levels me with a hard kiss all of a sudden that about knocks me over. It's so sudden and hot that it takes me a second to remember that I probably have the worst morning breath of all time. I cover my mouth quickly to prevent a repeat kiss, but he only laughs, kissing my hand in front of my mouth.

"Come on before those heathens eat everything. There's unfortunately probably a shit load of people who ended up passing out here or are still up and drinking from last night, so we'll have to battle them as well."

I roll my eyes at that last comment remembering how Jesse's directives were obeyed without question. I don't think anyone's about to swoop in and steal his food without permission. I see a smirk on his face out of the corner of my eye and know that he's thinking it was a ridiculous statement as well. It makes me smile even wider because I love Jesse's personality. I love all of their personalities. For someone who has spent her entire life hiding in the shadows, being around three men who are so confident and seem to hold the world in their hands is a whole new experience, but one that I love.

I hear the sound of Tanner's laugh as we walk down the stairs and I stop for a second, savoring the sound of it. Jesse pulls me along behind him after a moment. When we walk in, Tanner is getting a bunch of wrapped plates out of a large box that's giving off a heavenly smell.

"How did you get all of this delivered?" I ask in amazement as Tanner takes the foil off one of the plates and sets it down in front of me. It's so fresh that it's still steaming. It's piled high with all of my favorite breakfast foods; eggs, sausage and biscuits, and fresh fruit. I take a bite before anyone can answer and I let out a delighted moan as I savor the best biscuit I've ever tasted.

When I open my eyes, I see that all of the guys are staring at me. They look...hungry. "She just made that shit look like porn," says Jesse with a laugh. "We're definitely keeping her."

I blush at the connotation.

"In answer to your question, Tanner over here has an assistant that comes with the estate," says Jensen as he unwraps his own plate.

"Don't you mean the assistant that Tanner likes to screw when he's bored?" says a cruel voice that unfortunately ends up belonging to Reagan.

"I don't think you were invited," says Tanner coldly. Despite her bravado, Reagan shrivels with his tone.

"I thought we were supposed to talk. And besides, there isn't actually a list for your parties," she spits out. "Obviously there isn't a list, since someone let that trash in," she says, pointing at me.

Surprising myself, I don't let her words affect me and I continue to eat calmly knowing that one of the guys will deal with her. Tanner saunters over to her slowly, like a panther stalking his prey.

"Trash is an interesting word coming from you of all people," he says silkily.

"Didn't I hear you were with four guys last night?" asks

Jesse with a laugh. "They just waited outside the door for their turn. Didn't you do it right by the theatre room in hopes that Tanner would hear and get jealous?"

"Newsflash, sweetheart," adds Jensen. "You're nothing to him. You're nothing to any of us."

"Get out now," finishes Tanner. "And Reagan..." he says as she tries to flee the room. "Next time you try to talk to any of us, we'll act like you don't exist."

I finish my last bite of breakfast as she flies out of sight. I know I shouldn't feel satisfaction at what just happened, after all, it might happen to me someday. But it feels good for someone to stick up for me for once in my life. I don't feel alone anymore.

MONDAY COMES TOO SLOW. I had Jensen drop me off at the school after breakfast, telling him I had a project I had to work on so that he wouldn't try to drop me off at home and see my living conditions. The rest of the weekend is agonizingly lonely, which is strange considering I've spent my whole life alone and it's only been the last week that I've spent a significant amount of time with people at all. I didn't hear from the guys and tried not to think too hard about what that meant. No one drove by me as I walked to school Monday morning either, and I tried to prepare myself that they might have lost interest in me already.

Jesse's on time for our History class once again. He flashes me a grin as he saunters in but doesn't say anything to me during class. Amberlie shoots speculative looks at the two of us until I make a slashing motion across my neck signaling she needs to stop. Of course this just spurs her on and she spends the rest of class sending me notes asking about the party and my relationship with the guys.

I try to rush out of class, certain now that the guys are done with me, but Jesse stops me in the hallway before I can get anywhere. He cages me in against the lockers and my heart starts beating faster with his proximity. I inhale his sunshine scent, trying to calm down. Any chances of that disappear when I look up at him. He's staring down at me so intensely it feels like he can see into my soul. He hovers so close to me that our lips will brush if one of us moves even a little bit. I can't say that I didn't obsess over kissing him this weekend...obsess over kissing all of them again. The thought of how Jensen and Jesse's lips felt against mine haunted my dreams, making me feel slightly feverish twenty-four seven.

"Hey," he says, and the faint brush of his lips against mine make me feel like I'm about to faint. I plaster my head against the lockers, trying to get some space from him. He doesn't look the slightest bit perturbed that our lips just freaking touched.

"Hey," I whisper back, unable to speak any louder since I feel like I'm about to swallow my tongue.

"We're playing this local music festival this weekend and I want you to come," he says. I can see over Jesse's shoulder that there's what seems like a million people watching us in the hall, but it's hard to care when he's looking at me like this. Like I'm everything.

"Ok," I say dumbly. "What day are you playing?"

He flashes me a cheeky grin at my question, but his eyes tell a different story. They almost look tentative…

"We play on Sunday. We actually got picked to play when some of the bigger bands are playing, which is really cool…" He pauses, like he's weighing his next words. "But I was actually wondering if you wanted to go to some of the Saturday shows."

"Like with all of you?" I ask, still not understanding what he wants from me. He laughs at my question and leans in to erase the space I had put between us. Our noses touch and I shiver involuntarily as goosebumps erupt on my skin from the slight contact. My eyes keep flicking from his eyes to his full, pouty lips. I want to taste them again since our one kiss was so short and quick... I notice that his eyes are having trouble staying off my lips as well.

"Like with me," he says in a soft voice that makes me want to do whatever he wants. I stare at him, my face flushing. I want to ask if it's a date, but surely, it's not...right?

"Sounds good," I tell him, and his eyes lose that tentative look. They now look relieved. Did he actually think I would say no?

He moves away from me and starts walking backwards down the hallway, a grin on his face that I swear makes every girl he passes swoon. "So, it's a date?" he yells.

I blush and nod and he lets out a loud celebratory cry and a fist pump that ensures that absolutely everyone is looking at me. I lean back against the lockers and let out a loud exhale. Guess at least Jesse's not quite done with me.

I get through my next class and then walk to the lunch-room, unsure what to expect today. I'm surprised to see that Tanner is leaning against the wall at the entrance of the cafeteria, watching me as I walk down the hallway towards him.

"Hi Princess," he says, grabbing my waist and brushing a kiss on the top of my head. I savor his musky smell as I lean in towards him. "Can we talk for a second?" he asks after he pushes back from me to look into my eyes. Like Jesse this morning, he looks nervous...which makes me nervous. He takes my hand and leads me down the hallway into an empty classroom. I sit in one of the empty desks as he starts to pace back and forth in front of me.

"We never talked about what you saw Friday night," he says, running his hand aggressively through his hair.

I realize that he's talking about me seeing him doing drugs. This is definitely not a conversation I want to have with him. He must see my panicked expression because he starts to talk really fast.

"I just do it occasionally when I need to let off steam after a performance. I was really nervous when I saw you in the crowd and then afterward there was a group doing it and…" he rambles, but I cut him off.

"Are you trying to say that I'm the reason you snorted coke?" I ask him incredulously.

"Fuck, no that's not what I'm saying," he says frustratedly, grabbing his hair even harder and yanking it so hard I'm afraid that he's going to pull it out. "I'm just trying to tell you that I rarely do it. So, you don't have to be scared of me or whatever. I don't have a drug problem or anything," he says beseechingly.

I take a deep breath. "I'm sure that you've guessed just by my clothes that I don't have the same background as you." He opens his mouth, but I rush on, desperate to get it out. "What I haven't talked about at all except briefly to Jensen the other night…mostly because I don't talk to anyone about this, is that my home life is pretty crappy. My parents are both addicts in the worst way. Drugs, alcohol…you name it, they do it. I'm not going to tell you what to do, although I would rather you not snort cocaine…I just don't want you to be around me when you're using."

We're both quiet after my speech. Tanner looks conflicted, a mixture of shame and regret radiating across his features. "So, I guess I've ruined everything then, haven't I," he says, beginning to walk to the door. I stand up quickly.

"What are you talking about?" I ask him, rushing over to grab his hand.

"You just basically told me that I'm just like your parents," he says bitterly. "That doesn't bode well for a relationship."

I get stuck on his use of the word relationship but try to address the first sentence. "You aren't anything like my parents," I tell him soothingly. "I just don't want to be around you when you're doing drugs. There's no hidden message in my words."

He gets a determined look on his face and gives me a hard hug before leaning back to look down at me. "I won't do it anymore, so you won't have to worry about it," he says matter-of-factly. His previously pained expression relaxes, loosening the tiny lines around his eyes. It makes him look younger, more innocent.

"I'm not ever going to tell you what to do," I whisper even though I'm thrilled at the prospect of not having to worry about that with him.

After a minute, and because Tanner seems to need another one, I lay my forehead against his chest and breathe in his unique scent—clean sweat, musk, and maleness. He lays his cheek on my hair, and we stand there long enough that my stomach starts growling from hunger. But I stay still, enjoying a moment, a good one where the crushing weight of loneliness that I suspect we both feel a lot of the time, evaporates.

BETWEEN SCHOOL WORK and hanging out with the guys, the week flies by and before I know it, it's Friday. "So what time should I pick you up tomorrow?" Jesse asks after class, putting his arm around my shoulder like he loves to do. I have a momentary flash of panic thinking about him picking me up at the trailer. I may have given Tanner some details but I would rather keep the full scope of my problems away from all of them so I can at least have a bit more time with them thinking I'm normal. I'm sure Terry and David would pick the exact moment that Jesse arrived to start a brawl in the front room. I would never live it down.

"I'll meet you there," I tell him hurriedly, ducking under his arms to start for my next class since the bell was about to ring.

He looks disappointed at not being able to pick me up, but he wouldn't be if he realized what I was saving him from. "So tomorrow?" he yells down the hallway at my retreating back. The hallway erupts in gossip at his question. I throw a thumbs up over my shoulder like a complete nerd as I scurry away. I miss all of my calculus lecture and have to ask Amberlie for notes. The rest of the day passes in a blur. I don't see the other two members of the "hot squad" as I've been calling them in my head despite the fact that I keep an eye out for them. I inexplicably wish that they were all going to be there tomorrow.

I'm so distracted at the prospect of my outing with Jesse that I make the rookie mistake of walking into the trailer without scoping out the situation first. David is in the middle of rutting into one of the next-door neighbors while Terry lays passed out on the couch next to them, a syringe dangling from her hand. I'm frozen in shock for a second at the sight of so much nakedness and the fact that my step-father is literally fucking someone else in the same room as my passed-out mother. When David looks up at me with a disgusting smirk on his face, I come back to life and run out of the trailer, convinced that my brain is never going to be scrubbed free of that image for the rest of my life.

I'm shaking as I start to run as far from the trailer as I can get, not sure what I'm supposed to do. Without thinking, I automatically start dialing Jesse.

"Miss me already, pretty girl?" he asks when he answers.

"Are you busy right now?" I ask, trying to keep my voice steady as I put more distance between myself and the trailer park.

"What's wrong? Where are you? I'll come get you" he says, a sense of urgency in his voice at my obvious distress.

"Just past the mile marker 15 on the county road," I tell him, my voice hitching with relief that he's coming.

He must have been in the area because he finds me within ten minutes. I get inside his truck and he begins to drive. "Do you want to talk about it?" he asks.

"No," I whisper, tears starting to slide down my face at how crappy my parents were.

"Then we won't talk about it," he says, grabbing my hand and stroking it soothingly. I smile at him through the tears. We're quiet after that.

We drive for about fifteen minutes until he turns into a neighborhood that judging by the homes is obviously well to do, but not even close to the level of Tanner's wealth. He makes one more turn and then pulls into the driveaway of a traditional colonial red-brick mansion complete with white columns.

"Where are we?" I ask.

"My house," he says, turning off the truck. I start to panic at the prospect of meeting his parents. "Wow, pretty girl. Relax. My parents are gone for the weekend at one of my dad's conferences, so we'll have the whole house to ourselves unless my little sister decides to make an appearance. I wouldn't do that to you when you're so upset," he says sweetly, getting out of the truck and coming around to get me. He pulls me from the truck and into a hug so perfect that I can feel pieces of my cracked heart being stitched back together.

After probably five minutes passes, he begins to walk us into the house, still keeping a comforting arm around me. Jesse's house seems much more lived-in than Tanner's house. There's odds and ends strewn all about and as we walk through the kitchen there's snacks out on the counter and dishes in the sink. Everything about the home's decor is warm and welcoming. It's almost like you can feel that a really happy family lives here. Which I'm not sure is the case, but Jesse certainly seems to possess less demons than the other two by my observation so far. Looking around though, I wonder what inspired his nipple piercings. This is not a nipple piercing sort of background.

"Here's what we're going to do, Ari," he says, leading me into a tv room with a really comfy looking, worn couch and a projector screen almost as big as the one at Tanner's. "We're going to order some Chinese food, since I know you love that stuff. And then we're going to watch horrible romantic comedies that I'm sure you love because all girls seem to secretly love that shit. And we're not going to talk about anything."

My eyes start to well up at his proclamation. "That sounds perfect," I tell him as he leads me to the couch, probably unsure at this point I can walk by myself since I'm such a mess.

We spend the evening just as he described- stuffing ourselves with Orange Chicken and Chow Mein, and binge watching every rom-com that Jesse can find on Netflix. It's so perfect that I fall right to sleep cuddled in his arms without one thought of the horror that had happened earlier.

THE NEXT MORNING, I wake up before Jesse and savor the feeling of his hard, warm body against mine. One of his legs is hitched over my hips so we're as close as possible and his head is buried in my neck. It somehow manages to be comfortable despite the fact that I can feel something hard and long pushing against my stomach. Jesse begins to stir a few minutes later as the sun streaming in through one of the back windows starts to fill the whole room with light.

He shifts, moving his face from my neck as his eyes slowly blink open. I stare at them mesmerized. I once read that some scientists believe that you can fall in love with someone just by looking into their eyes long enough. I scoffed at it then...but now I kind of get it. I blame his beautiful sky-blue eyes for the way that I'm feeling right now. They are endless pools of possibility and I can see a chance of happiness in their depths.

"Hi, pretty girl," he says in a low, gruff voice. He brushes a kiss across my lips. It feels more comforting than sexual and I wonder what it would feel like to wake up to such a kiss for the rest of my life. "Are you excited for today?" he asks in a way that I know is asking more if I'm up for the concert than anything else.

"Yes," I tell him with a smile. "I think it's going to be a perfect day."

"I think so too," he says, his eyes running all over my face in a way that makes me wonder what he's looking for.

We lay there for a few minutes more, both in no hurry to unwrap ourselves from each other. When we do get up, we make breakfast together in the kitchen and I help him take care of his dog, a giant, loveable beast of a retriever that is as obsessed with Jesse as I'm beginning to be.

Afterwards he leads me to his little sister's room, and we raid her closet. I feel a little weird borrowing from a girl I haven't even met, but Jesse assures me that she has so many clothes that she won't miss anything. The size of her closet doesn't dispute that. I find a pair of skinny jeans that fits me better than anything I own, a vintage looking Guns N' Roses tank, and a black zip-up jacket that couldn't be better suited for a concert. At least they look like something people probably wear to regular concerts where they aren't trying to get into the singers' pants like everyone was yesterday. After slipping on my boots that I was luckily wearing the day before, I'm ready to go.

On the way to the music festival Jesse explains that this is a yearly event that seems to be getting bigger and bigger. As he talks about what bands are going to be there, I can see how excited he is to get to perform alongside them. We get to the park where it's being held, and I see hundreds of people walking towards a large stage that is set up in the distance. They are all carrying blankets and coolers, which has me panicking for a second thinking that we didn't bring either until Jesse grabs a few blankets from the backseat and hands them to me before pulling out a large cooler from the bed of the truck. I laugh a bit giddily at how prepared he is for this. I find myself hoping that we can stay all day until the last band finishes their set. I don't think I could ever get tired of being around him.

He grabs the blankets and throws them on the cooler which has wheels that allow him to easily pull it behind us. He takes my hand in his free hand, entwining our fingers. He walks more closely beside me and we both slow our steps, his fingers squeezing mine. My hand is warmed by his, by knowing that he wanted connection just as much as I did. I never thought I would be a hand holder, but I sure did love holding hands with all of them.

"You know I actually come by myself to this every year," he says as we walk. "I've never told the guys that, and hell maybe they do it too for all I know. But I've never seen them here."

"Why did you ask me to come if you like to come alone?" I ask curiously.

"I couldn't get it out of my head," he says. "I just knew that you would make it even better." He grins sheepishly. "Jensen might have also told me how much you like music so I thought I would win some brownie points for taking you to listen to music on our first date."

I laugh hard at his admission. But it abruptly stops when I wonder what else the guys have shared. I'll just have to expect it going forward that what I tell one of them will probably be told to the rest. Tanner had probably already mentioned what I had told him about my family the other night and that's why Jesse didn't press me to talk about it. Oh well, I wasn't going to worry about it.

Looking around, I was shocked at how many people were here. Bellmont wasn't a very large town, but there were five other neighboring towns that worked together to help bring this festival here. Jesse paid a $20 fee for each of us as we walk in, and I panicked a bit that he just spent that much money on me. The cost didn't seem to faze him so I decided not to say anything so I didn't make anything awkward. After paying the fee, we walked towards the stage. I could hear the sound check up ahead.

When we reached the field in front of the stage, Jesse leads me to the left of the stage, where he explains he thinks there are the best acoustics in relations to the trees. I help him spread out the larger blanket and plop down, both of us turning on our sides to face one another. The first band was still setting up, so we had time to talk. Once the music started, I was sure it would be too loud to hear each other without yelling.

"I'm so glad you're here," he says sweetly, scooting closer

to me. "I hope you like the music. There are usually a lot of covers but some of the original stuff usually blows me away too."

"I'm sure I will," I tell him, unable to hold in the grin on my face. He pushes the hair away from my shoulder. My jacket slips over my shoulder with the movement and Jesse wastes no time running his fingers over the bare skin.

"I can't not touch you. I'm not going to be sorry for it either."

I raise an eyebrow. "Did you see me complaining?" I ask, reaching out to grab a handful from the center of his shirt. I pull him closer. "I don't like the space between us," I admit.

I prop myself up on one arm and look down at him. His head is cushioned on his bent arm, his biceps flexed from the positioning. His golden hair is deliciously mussed up and his lips are in a contented smile. That smile is one of my favorites, knowing that I helped put it there. I felt bold in that moment. I could see how happy he was, and it gave me courage to make a move.

I lean down, allowing my hair to become a curtain around us, nuzzling my nose against his. I could tell that he was holding back, allowing me to take control of this situation. I pepper his scruff covered chin with kisses, loving the bite against my lips. I kiss his lips quickly once, and then twice, and when I try to pull away the third time, his hands come up and hold my head in place, kissing me at his leisure. He's careful not to move too fast as if he doesn't want to scare me.

Not sure about the PDA that was allowed at the park, I pull away and off of him and lay flat on my back. I blow out an exaggerated breath.

"Does it always feel like this?" I ask without thinking.

"No. I can say that it definitely does not always feel like

this. In fact, I'd go as far as to say it never feels like this, or at least it never has for me before."

I turn my eyes to his. His eyes are running over my face. It makes me feel self-conscious.

"Why do you look at me like that?"

His eyes meet mine. "I'm memorizing your face." He says it nonchalantly, as if that was the most obvious answer. Before I could ask why, the music starts, drowning out my voice. We both turn our heads to the stage to listen. At some point, Jesse curls up behind me, allowing me to use his arm as a pillow, his other hand running down my waist, over the curve of my hip. Some of the songs, he uses my hip as a guitar, plucking his fingers against the material in time to the band. I was sure it was innocent, but the repetitive motion was driving me crazy. As a result, we make out for all of the songs, pausing to catch our breaths, laugh, or have a sip of soda. Being around Jesse was like being alive. I was more aware of my heart beating, I was challenged to evaluate myself, and I laughed so often my cheeks hurt. When the third band played and Jesse and I had each finished our second sodas, the sky had grown dark. The only lighting was around the stage and on the road, leaving those of us on the grass in complete darkness.

When the band played a song that was a bit sappy but still upbeat, Jesse hopped up to his feet and reached a hand down to me.

"What are you doing?" I asked, suspicious.

"I, Jesse Carroway, am asking you, Ariana Kent, to dance with me on the most perfect date in the history of the world," he says with a dramatic bow. He seems almost euphoric, and while I want to protest, I find myself placing my hand in his and standing up. He leads me towards the tree line, completely out of sight from the other concert-goers. It is absolutely black except for the stage, so I take comfort in knowing that no one else can see us. We could live in this square of trampled grass off to the side of the actual concert, and only acknowledge each other. Jesse dances with me in time to the beat of a cover of Rihanna's "We Found Love" in the grass, spinning me away from him and pulling me back with drama. Our dancing doesn't go with the beat of the song at all but it's happy and perfect and fits the mood of our night together.

The song blends into the next one. "Imagine Dragons," I whisper, my lips against his hair. "I love this band." I feel his lips touch the shell of my ear as he sings along with the lyrics to "Bad Liar." He serenades me in the dark, his hips pressed against mine, the hand he holds to my back tenderly tracing my spine. Every few chords, he presses his lips to my earlobe, in a kiss as soft as his voice. He doesn't withhold anything from me, whether it's his words or even his touch. He gives me everything. And for the first time in my life, I fall in love. I fall in love with his hand on my waist, under the stars, while we danced to borrowed words. I fall in love with his breath at my ear, his cheek pressed against mine, with his body pressed tightly to mine. I fall in love again when we lay on the ground, my head on his chest and his hand in my hair. His heart beating in my ear was the loudest sound, my favorite sound. Not for the first time, I knew I was in trouble.

That was unexpected. I can still feel Tanner's lips against mine. They feel bruised, tender, swollen from his affection. I'd never been kissed like that before. There had never been that level of passion between us before they left. Why did he just kiss me? Pulling myself from the wall, my legs shaking even more than before, I stupidly walk back down the hallway, unable to stay away from him after that even if he was done with me. I once again pause at the entrance of the green room and stare at Tanner who is now talking to a gorgeous redhead as if he hadn't just been in a dark room with me eating me alive.

I watch Tanner flirt with the trashy redhead from the shadows right outside the room. I feel absurdly jealous and it only grows as she lays a hand on his chest that he doesn't shrug away. How I'm feeling reminds me of when I had decided to cut myself off from all things Sounds of Us. I had managed to go a year without looking them up, but one night, in a fit of self-destructive misery I had given in to the urge to read every damn thing about them, thinking if I knew all their move on. It didn't. I absorbed story upon story and pictures of them gallivanting around the world, always with a flock of trashy girls around them. And even years since they had been mine, I still had felt possessive over them even then.

I want to march in right now and claim what's mine, but I don't. I don't want to chance an encounter with Jesse and Jensen before I've calmed down. And what I'm feeling right now is the opposite of calm. Obviously, since I'm using ridiculous words like "mine" in relation to Tanner. Tanner keeps glancing at the doorway and I absurdly hope that he's looking for me, that he feels the same pull that I do to be near him now that we have reunited.

It turns out that I was keeping watch in the wrong direction if I was really hoping to avoid Jensen and Jesse. A door opens right across from my hiding place and Jesse walks out, shirtless like the rockstar he is, singing softly to himself. It's too late for me to hide and my eyes catch his from across the hallway. I hold his gaze as regret rolls through my stomach. I think of words spoken as truth—an echo of the soul.

He's beautiful, and guilt for thinking so works my stomach into a knot. I have no right to him. I slide my gaze to his bare chest. The perfect skin is broken by a smattering of new tattoos and his familiar, still delicious nipple piercings. He's wearing a pair of black jeans that are much too low to be decent. I shake my head to adjust my thoughts. A few days ago, Jesse was the last person I'd thought I would ever see again. Today, I'm enjoying the fuck out of the picture-perfect sight before me. And that sums it up; one decision changes lives. One act, one moment, alters the course of many. One decision certainly altered the course of my life.

I pull my hands to my temples, rubbing them as he walks to stand in front of me. My phone starts ringing, and it tumbles out of my hand as I drop it. It clatters at our feet as he grabs my shirt and tips my head back, so I have no choice but to look into his glistening eyes. I have never seen pain like this before, but if that word could manifest itself into a picture it would be Jesse in this moment.

"You promised," he says quietly in a tone heavy with betrayal and anger.

It was a vow I had no right to make. A promise broken. A life lost. I blink against his animosity and accept the accusation. I can't speak as to what happened. Putting a voice to it will bring that one night to life, and I won't have him carry the details of that burden. It belongs solely to me.

Despite my fault, I'm the one who starts crying. Indecision crosses his face and then it seems like he's unable to stop himself as he wraps me in his arms. Being in his arms again feels like coming home. It's a relief that angers me because it tells me that I'm weak, that I'll never be able to move on from this fantasy I've built up in my head about them. I didn't want to be held like some baby who needed comfort. I couldn't stand his pity a moment longer, and I begin to push him away.

And then everything shifts.

His shoulders sag, and his back curves out as his head slides down to my shoulder. He turns his face into my neck and … he clings to me.

"Do you hate me?" I whisper into his hair as I take a deep breath of that sunshine smell that still radiates off of him even now. He pulls away from me, staring at me as if he's memorizing my face like he used to do all those years before.

"If I end up hating you, it would be easier," he spits out. "Please. Please make me hate you. Why don't you just finish the job so I can get on with my life!" he pleads with me.

His eyes blaze against mine, daring me to do my worst, even though my worst has already been done. My hands shake. Jesse grabs my face with both hands. His mouth crashes down on mine as he kisses me fiercely. His tongue pushes between my lips, tangling with my own. He groans and flattens me against the wall. He releases my face and captures my wrists, holding them above my head as his body pummels me with the force of his hunger. I'm on fire. His and Tanner's touch has awakened every cell in my body I thought was dead. Just as I start to kiss him back, he lets me go and backs away, visibly struggling to control himself.

He drags his finger through his previously perfectly styled blonde hair. "Fuck, you still drive me crazy," Jesse mutters, breathing heavily.

Until this moment, I didn't know how much I'd needed him to need me, but it unravels as a heavy ball in my stomach to realize that he still does. That thought confuses me, or maybe it doesn't. I've been dazed for so many years—feeling needed has been the last thing on my radar.

Jesse

What I remember as the angular lines of her face are softened around her cheekbones and jaw. Ariana had been a breathtakingly attractive teenager...but as a woman? As a woman her otherworldly beauty robs me of coherent thought. She has the face of an angel; impossibly long, dark lashes framed unusual caramel eyes under perfectly arched brows. Her delicate nose tilted up pertly above full pillowy lips, and her oval face was graced with high cheekbones. Creamy skin, hair the color of dark mahogany and seductively wavy, I want to dig my fingers in her glorious tresses just so I can tilt her head to gaze upon her face. Every love song that I had written for our band was inspired by her to this day. Her arresting beauty has haunted me since we parted and seeing this grown up version of her will haunt my dreams for the rest of my life if she leaves me again.

She's wearing my favorite leather skirt and it showcases perfectly how the lean shape of her body has fleshed into soft curves. Her tight shirt accentuates the breadth of her stomach and the swell of her tits. I want so badly to look away, to concentrate on anything but her, yet even if I try, I'm drawn back in. She's a fucking projectile burning through my atmosphere with enough force to leave me winded. She's more than sexy. She's light and dark at the same time, dark hair and eyes the color of eternity. This woman is not just a moment in time, but all of them brought together. The kind you give your soul to and then rest your head at ease. She's endless, and most certainly has always been my undoing.

The refined elegance of her posture speaks to an upbringing far greater than the dregs of small-time, small-town South Carolina. Ariana may be small, but she's fierce. The sly tilt of her head and the way she looks down her nose could be intimidating for some. Not to me. Looking at her, it takes everything I have to prevent myself from admitting that I haven't been able to get on with my life, that I wasn't over her.

The way that she's looking at me, I can tell that she's afraid of the depth of the feelings in my eyes. But I can't stop myself from what I feel just by seeing her again. However, I'm also desperately aware that she could run away from me at any second and that I need to slow the fuck down if I want her to stay. I take her hand in mine. My huge grip engulfs hers and a warm feeling tickles up my arm just by feeling her skin against mine.

"Have you eaten yet?" I ask, watching as a surprised look crosses her face.

She shakes her head no. I tap the VIP badge she's wearing around her neck, her face blushes as I graze her perfect breasts.

It's the same glorious color as the blush she used to get when we were younger. It gives me a sense of satisfaction that at least one thing hasn't changed about her.

"This comes with a pretty awesome meal if you're hungry," I say, trying to sound innocent although the boob graze was definitely on purpose.

She nods and since I still haven't let go of her hand, I start to pull her behind me into the green room, despite the obvious reluctance I can feel in her body. It's amazing how just holding her hand is sparking a million memories of my life before now.

As I walk in, Tanner looks over, his eyes glued to Ariana. There's a hard, desperate longing in his gaze and I wonder if they already had their reunion and it hadn't gone well. I lead her over to him, nevertheless, not paying any mind to his flavor of the week and longtime drug dealer, Tanya, who's desperately hanging off of him. The girl doesn't know what's coming now that Tanner's "Princess" has returned.

"Tanner, you remember Ari," I say jokingly. Ariana's gripping my hand like it's her lifeline and the protective streak she always brought out of me urges me to drag her away from the uncomfortable situation. But then I remember how she basically ruined my life for the last five years and I don't feel so bad about torturing her a little. It's amazing how having her back for fifteen minutes makes me want to forget all the heartache and indescribable pain she put me through. I can't forget it though. She could easily do it again. And this time I might not be able to recover.

Tanner doesn't answer me, instead he starts to nibble on Tanya's neck, his eyes glued to Ariana's as he does so. She looks sick to her stomach as she watches Tanner and I finally give in to the roaring inside of me that's always been desperate to make her smile, and I pull her away from Tanner's little game of vengeance. There is a table in the back of the room that's laden with food as well as about twenty other VIP guests who are eyeing me like they are lions and I'm particularly tasty meat.

I give them the stage smile that I've perfected and make sure to greet them, never letting Ari go. If she's going to be in our life she will have to get used to this part of the job. Most VIPs are actually not too bad. They're usually on the younger side and have gotten the tickets for them and twenty of their friends for a birthday present from their rich father. They usually can't get a word out because they are in shock and if you take a quick picture with them and give them a hug, they're pretty much guaranteed to be your fans for the rest of your life. There are however some VIPs that are nothing but groupies, like the one trying to push my hand onto her heaving double ds despite the fact that I'm obviously with Ari at the moment. I slept with my fair share in the first few tours, desperate to try and fuck Ari out of my mind. When it didn't work and I realized how miserable it was making me feel, I backed off and haven't touched one in over a year.

I manage to wrench my hand from the girl's and make it to the table where I start stacking two plates. I feel a sick sense of dread when I realize that I've loaded up Ari's entire plate with what used to be her favorite foods. What's it going to mean for me that I'm still so gone over this girl that I can remember everything about her? Looking over at her, she's looking at the plate like it's a snake that is about to bite her. I'm sure we're both wondering how our habits have survived five years apart from each other. I throw the plates down and garner a sweet gasp from her when I yank her towards the door that leads to my dressing room. What I'm feeling feels too personal to be on display in front of a room full of strangers even if they are all going to think I'm taking her inside to fuck her.

She gives a soft sob when she sees the intensity in my eyes

after we get inside and the door is shut. "What do you want, Jesse?" she asks, which angers me because it should be fucking apparent what I want, what I've always wanted from her.

"I have never wanted anything more than you." I tell her. "I haven't—I've never thought about kissing someone the way I want to with you. And fucking shit, I want to worship every part of your body, but I also want to fuck hard and raw until your sweet voice is rough from begging and then we'll begin again. Just us. Starting with a kiss." My hand trembles when it reaches her nape, winding through her soft hair. "Let me in."

ARIANA

Jesse gives me hope. Faith in tomorrow, trust in the future, and freedom to feel everything that I thought was lost. To feel with him. With Jesse.

"Yes."

At the one-word submission, he hisses and then dips down. He aligns his mouth with my own, and we kiss. We kiss until breathing is forgotten, catching only short gasps of air when we part long enough to move a fraction. We drown in the thundering rain that is our pulse and the beat of what becomes us. We kiss until the palate of colors creating his canvas blends into mine and a new picture forms. We kiss until our souls bleed from the pain and heal into a new and beautiful masterpiece. And then the silence that surrounds us is quiet serenity. It ends on a heady moan, his or mine, both, when reality intrudes from voices in the outside room.

Jesse pulls away but he doesn't go far, leaning his forehead against mine. "Where have you been the last five years?" he asks, and I know he isn't asking a question about geography, he's asking a question about my heart. Fear shocks my system as I remember the phone call that came in when I first saw Jesse. I'm sure it was Gentry. Jesse mistakes my look and abruptly pulls away from me.

A tremor bursts across his shoulders, and he grabs his hair. Bending over at the waist, he groans. I fight the urge to go to him, to say I'm sorry and I didn't mean it, and that we're good together, because we were, we are, but then he stands and his eyes cool to an icy blue. With a nod, he slams a hand into his jeans pocket. "I'm sorry I burdened you with my feelings."

"That isn't . . ." I try to tell him, but just then the door opens and Jensen fills the doorway, taking my breath away.

For one heartbeat, pain burns through the hard veneer sculpting Jensen's features, pain and sorrow, like a man who knows too much and can't wade through his mucky memories. He drowns under the burden.

"Jensen," I whisper and reach for him. The pain melts away, leaving a blank mask.

"We're on in ten," he says to Jesse, slamming the door behind him without another look.

Jesse starts to walk towards the door. "We'll talk after the show," he says, and then he too leaves the room.

It feels odd knowing that he just left me in his dressing room. I had always imagined that the stars' dressing rooms would look like something out of the page of a design magazine, but this room looks just like Jesse. There are clothes sprawled all over the floor, I'm not sure what from since he just left for the show still just in a pair of black jeans. There are some empty Snickers' wrappers laying on the coffee table along with a few empty cans of Mountain Dew. Walking over to a mirror vanity on the side of the room, I pick up the lone picture frame sitting on it. My hands begin to tremble as I see that it's one of the four of us. It must have been taken right before they left although I don't remember it. I'm smiling widely at whoever was taking the picture. It's a real smile stemming from something one of the guys had just said. What strikes me most about the picture is that while I'm looking straight at the camera, all of the guys are looking straight at me. I had never seen this picture before, and I want to steal it and hoard it away so I can never forget that I was once adored.

Setting the picture down despite my baser urge, I walk out of Jesse's dressing room, closing the door softly behind me. So far, the night has been a lesson in agony but I need to snap out of the melancholy I'm feeling and just try to live in the moment since I'll never get it back.

Jesse's sitting on a stool, talking to a now red-headless Tanner. He glances up as I walk closer, blinking away his vulnerability and hiding behind the whiskey bottle he has in his hands. He takes a long swallow. A sliver of pain slides through his sky-blue eyes but another long swig follows, dimming the light. Brushing the back of his hand across his lips, he flicks his gaze at Tanner, and then a blonde sneaks into his side to whisper in his ear. Bitter resentment roars to life in my chest, and I hate it. I hate that I feel something in this moment. Tears rush my eyes, but I bat my lashes and force my focus to examining the rest of the room.

When I look back at Jesse, the blonde is looking at me, a speculative look on her face. She flips her hair. I flip mine. She smirks. I smirk. She laughs. I laugh. She touches. I—that's taking things too far. Before I can go after her though, there's a silky voice in my ear.

"Want to get out of here?" it asks, a large hand landing on my hip. Everything after that is a blur. Jensen has the guy by the neck, and his voice sends chills down my spine. "Hands off what's mine, Levi."

"Fuck you, Jensen!" says the red-faced guy who I've never seen before. That's all it takes. One angry-as-hell rockstar and every pair of eyes in the room rushes our way. Levi suddenly twists out of Jensen's grip and shoves. Jensen's thigh crumbles, and he uses a table to catch his fall, cracking the leg. His eyes flame wide. He lunges.

Tanner steps in. One fist coils in Levi's shirt, the other in Jensen's. "Cool it. We need to get out on stage right now," Tanner snarls.

Jesse's blue eyes find mine for a second. Is that sympathy? Then he turns to follow Jensen and Tanner out of the room towards the stage. I'm left with the carnage: a broken table and my scattered breath.

Levi leaves the room with a backwards glare at me. Giving him a second to get farther away, I collect myself and then follow the line of VIPs out to the specially marked area of the front row that's been reserved for us. Somehow, I end up in the front of the dead center of the stage.

The stadium goes dark, and the crowd erupts in a fervent cheer. Thousands of chesty girls scream to be noticed as the band walks on stage, only their silhouettes visible to the crowd against the crush of the lights. My heart pounds as Tanner takes the stage and picks up his first guitar. Without saying a word, he busies himself studying the strings, double-checking the tuning. Behind him, Jensen starts strumming the opening beats to their most recent single, "Cry For You." Off to the side of the stage, a musician who is not an original member of Sounds of Us starts the opening piano notes and Jesse kicks in on the drums. The music swells until it reaches a feverish pitch. Finally, the lights focus, fully revealing Tanner as he saunters to the microphone and begins to sing.

"You stole my heart, left me to die, you took my breath, you made me cry. But I'm done with that, I'm done with your games, this much is true. I'm never again, going to cry for you..."

The crowd loses it. I can't take my eyes off him. Every fiber in his being oozes charisma. Every movement is personified charm. It must be impossible for anyone in this stadium not to have a crush on him, a crush on all of them. As I watch I can't help but drift into the memory of the first show I saw them perform. Remembering his expressive eyes and the control he possesses over the muscles in his face, I blush at the memory even now. I allow myself to rerun that entire first show in my head and marvel. As the song ends, he removes his guitar strap from his shoulder, and instead of putting the instrument back on its stand, he lays it down on the floor in the middle of the stage and turns to greet the crowd.

A frantic guitar tech gives an I-know-he-does-that-just-to-mess-with-me eye roll and inconspicuously runs out on stage to save the stranded piece of equipment, then places an acoustic guitar on the stand. Tanner rips off his shirt making the whole stadium roar and then switches spots with Jesse. As he walks to the drums, I gape at his body along with every other person in the crowd. His back is smooth but for cut bunches of muscle that roll and dip in all the right places. I'm not so stuck on those, but the tattoos that cover one side of him from hip through to sleeve, leaving the other side of his back as unmarked as it was the day he was born. Two sides of a coin, perfectly delineated by his spine. Angel wings and words, tribal markings and Celtic knots, all woven together in a masterpiece painted on his skin even though I know they're hiding a multitude of scars. It's beautiful. He's beautiful.

I swallow and tuck my chin to my chest, shocked by the increased speed of my pulse, my breath, and the stirrings of other long-forgotten human needs.

"Hello," Jesse greets the crowd as they erupt in deafening noise. From my vantage point, I watch as the lights illuminate the thousands of faces before us. Girls swoon while their boyfriends try to appear unaffected. Jesse looks over at Jensen, who's dressed up a lot more than the other guys in his navy blazer with elbow patches over a t-shirt. They smile at each other in a shared moment, seeming to know the other so well they can communicate without words. Jensen shoots me a glance in the crowd and a thrill of unease hits my stomach as Jesse turns back to the crowd.

"We're going to take you back in time, with some songs off our first album," he says into the microphone, as he picks up the acoustic and strums a few chords. Tanner chimes in with his hint of an accent, "if you're thinking this is about you, it is," he jokingly says and the crowd laughs, even though I know the truth laced in his words.

Jesse's shoulders hunch forward as he launches into "Promises," the third single from their first album. I hate this song. Even though he performs it beautifully, every word is a bite into my heart as it tells the story of the lying bitch, me, who broke all her vows to the boys she loved.

The crowd doesn't share my hatred of the song and sings along with unabashed abandon. Jesse looks down at me while he sings the song, and despite the nastiness of the song, I feel intimately connected to Jesse in that moment, like we share a secret.

The show boulders on, and the guys all work the stage, throwing their entire body into every motion. They are all exemplary performers; they pull out all the stops. As a band, Sounds of Us is in perfect sync. Their group energy is contagious, and they move as one, dancing around the stage and encouraging the crowd. However, I wish that their energy wasn't devoted to pounding in my head every lyric that testifies just how much they hate me, how much I ruined everything, how much I broke their hearts. Song after song makes sure that I can't miss their message.

They quake into the grand finale, lights blazing and drums crashing in a final crescendo. Back at the drums for the last few songs, Jesse throws his drumsticks into the crowd, and the band exits the stage as the masses cry for more. As for me, I just cry.

10
THEN

"**W**e did it," Tanner says as he rushes into the room, immediately grabbing me and spinning me around. "Brandon just called with the news. We're going to L.A. to record our album," he tells me. His face is glowing, and I want to capture a picture of his happiness so that I can carry it with me always.

"That's amazing," I tell him, burying my face in his neck and breathing in his scent. They've worked so hard for this. I always knew it would happen for them. How could it not with how talented they are? There was nobody like them.

"When do you leave?" I ask breathlessly, lifting my head to peer into his silver eyes. They're framed by long dark lashes that would make any girl jealous and the rest of the package is just as gorgeous. All three of my boys are beautiful, but Tanner was definitely the one you could classify as "pretty boy" handsome. Tall, sexy, and confident, with just a touch of a British accent in his smoky voice, my heart always felt like it was about to beat out of my chest whenever he was looking at me.

"Friday," he tells me with a broad grin that never ceases to take my breath away. It dims after a moment. We both realize at that same time that I still have a whole semester left of school. I won't be able to go with them like we've always talked about until it's done.

"We can tell them we had something come up, that we have to delay for a few months," he says, trying to pretend like what he's saying is a possibility, like that wouldn't mean the death knell for their career before it even began. I wouldn't let them fail because of me.

"Four months will fly by," I whisper, smoothing down a section of his hair that was trying to fly away. "We'll talk every day. You won't even have time to miss me." I smile tremulously, feeling my eyes start to water as I think about them leaving me behind. They were my whole life and had been for over a year.

But I could do this. They had been taking care of me since I moved here, I could take care of myself for four months.

Tanner takes my chin gently in his and tips up my face so I'm looking at him. My mouth begins to water being this close to him. "Ari…" he begins before the door crashes open and Jesse and Jensen come stalking into the room, their gazes both intent on me.

Like always, there seems to be less oxygen in the room when the three of them are all in it. Sometimes it's hard to remember that life isn't just about them. They're a force of energy that pushes out anyone and anything. I couldn't remember what it was like when they weren't around me.

"What's wrong with her?" barks Jensen, and I can't help but smile. Jensen is my protector, willing to do anything to make me happy, even if he has to go against one of the guys. He's also the one that has always been able to see right through me. He'll be the hardest to convince that I'll be alright when they're gone.

"Nothing's wrong," I tell him with a slow smile. It's slow

because I can't summon up the happiness necessary for a quick one. "We were just celebrating the news. I'm so proud of you guys," I tell them, the end of my voice tailing into a squeak. I bury my head in Jensen's shoulder so the guys can't see my face. I need to get it together if I'm not going to ruin their lives like I have with everyone else that's ever known me.

Jensen sticks his face in my hair, inhaling in the way that makes me feel like I'm his favorite scent in the world. I abruptly get pulled away.

"Hey, I signed with a label too," says Jesse teasingly as he pulls me into a hug. Of the three of them, Jesse is the one that's always quick to smile. He sees the sunny side of every situation and I desperately need his light right now. I inhale the hint of sunshine that always radiates off of him as he pulls me close, already thinking of what it will be like when I don't get it every day.

"It will just be a few months, pretty girl," he whispers to me in his honey-coated voice and just like always he manages to pull a real smile from me.

I pull away from him reluctantly and nod. "Are you practicing today?" I ask, wanting to change the subject and have at least one more normal day before my whole world changes.

"We have to. The label is expecting us to be ready to record the second we land in L.A." says Tanner. My heart leaps. Just hearing the words label and record in L.A. sends flutters all over my body. It's really happening.

The next couple of hours pass and we all seem to have the same idea of pretending that it's just our usual Wednesday. I sit quietly on the faded leather couch in the corner where I usually do homework while they rehearse. Today I can only pretend, however. I'm already thinking about how I'm going to have to start playing their CDs while I work after they leave.

I've gotten so used to their voices being the soundtrack of my math and English homework that I'm not sure I can actually do my homework assignments without their songs.

Thirty minutes goes by and the little garage where they practice starts to fill up. Looking around dazedly I realize that quite a few of the kids from school showed up to watch them practice. Word must have gotten out that they were leaving, the crowd is twice as large as usual.

Karmen, a girl I have the unfortunate privilege of going to school with, sidles up next to the couch and sits down. I look at her annoyed, everyone knows this is my domain during the guys' practices.

"So, I heard that the guys are leaving you behind," she says to me in a voice that's meant to sound sympathetic but instead comes across bitchy. I know her too well at this point not to know that she's trying to make me feel like crap.

"I'll be joining them after school," I tell her, not sure why I sound like I'm trying to convince myself that what I'm saying is true.

"How long do you think they're going to let you hang on to their coattails?" she asks offhandedly. "You know that when there's a million girls vying for their attention, they won't be content settling for just one." Her comment manages to hit too close to how I actually feel for comfort. I say nothing, choosing to simply roll my eyes at her in response. The eye roll is meant to come across as confident, but my insides are in turmoil as I roll her words around my head. When will the guys start thinking of me as the burden they picked up accidently and can't get rid of? What will I do then? We technically still aren't anything but friends. There's been a lot of kissing and they're constantly touching me, but there hasn't been anything else despite the fact that I've been dying for more. How could I even expect them to want me around when we're technically not even together?

"Ready to go?" asks Jesse, sidling up to me and throwing his arm over my shoulder as is his habit. I realize that they're done, and Tanner and Jensen are finishing putting away the equipment. Jesse's a bit sweaty from playing but I don't mind, the boy pulls off sweat very well.

"Ariana and I were just talking about how excited she is to meet up with you in L.A.," says Karmen in a falsely sweet voice. Jesse looks at me, his eyes glimmering, he knows exactly how I feel about Karmen and her antics.

"We'll be counting down the days," he says, brushing a soft kiss against my forehead that makes my entire body tingle. I forget all about Karmen and her wicked tongue as he takes my hand and leads me to where Tanner and Jensen are now waiting by the door, talking to a few of their college class-mates. Jensen places his hand on my lower back when we get to them and my body seems to feel like it's on overload. The guys give me the simplest touches, but every day it seems to mean more. How am I going to live without it?

After grabbing a pizza, we head to the guys' apartment right outside of the Bellmont University campus. The guys are freshman there, one year ahead of me. This last year of high school has been miserable without them. I've been tempted just to drop out and get my GED, but my fears of ending up like my mother have stopped me from doing anything rash.

We eat and sit around the tv talking about what L.A. is going to be like. The label is setting them up with an apart-ment right outside of the studio and they're teasing me about how they are going to decorate my room before I get there. There's a sadness permeating the room despite Tanner and Jensen's attempt at levity. The guys are nursing beers, and I'm laying with my head in Tanner's lap. I look over at Jesse who's been oddly quiet all night. He's usually the one who would be cracking the most jokes, but instead he's staring at the television, lost in thought. I get up and surprise him when I get in his lap and wrap my arms around his neck. It's taken a year for me to feel comfortable touching them first, but now that I've started doing it, it's like I can't stop myself from doing it all the time. The guys haven't seemed to mind.

"What are you thinking about?" I whisper in his ear, grazing my lips against it. He shivers and I feel him start to harden under me. I see the other two pointedly averting their eyes away from Jesse and I and focusing on the tv where a basketball game just started.

"I'm thinking this is bullshit. You should just transfer to a high school in L.A. and graduate there. I don't like the idea of you staying here. What if something happens?"

It's something that I've thought about since I heard the news, but there's always the risk that my credits wouldn't transfer and Amberlie would probably kill me if she had to finish senior year without me, even if I've spent almost all my time with the guys lately. There's also the part of me that wants them to really be able to concentrate on recording their album without me distracting them. But I can't tell him that because he would immediately tell me how crazy I was and how I wouldn't distract them at all.

The prospect of them leaving is scary for another reason though. Terry and David have been getting even worse over the past year and I've had to spend more and more nights at the guys' apartment when things were too dangerous for me to stay at my trailer. Terry had even been hospitalized for overdosing a few months ago. Without the guys here, I'll have to find somewhere else to go when things get really bad. Jesse had promised me that his family had already agreed to take me in at any time and I knew Amberlie's family would do the same, but there was just something so safe about how the guys made me feel.

I lean my forehead against Jesse's, soaking in the feel of his skin against mine.

"I have an idea!" Jesse announces abruptly, lifting me as he stands up. I automatically wrap my legs around him. He spins me around and makes me laugh before talking again. Tanner and Jensen look at him expectantly.

"We've got three nights left before we leave. Let's each spend one night alone with Ari until then."

"We all get days though," says Jensen. "I don't want to miss seeing her for two out of the three days."

"Agreed," says Tanner, his silver eyes warming up as he looks at the sliver of skin that's appeared from my position around Jesse's waist.

"Um, is anyone going to ask me if that's all right?" I ask jokingly.

"My apologies, pretty girl," Jesse says sarcastically. "Is my plan acceptable to you?" he says with a smirk.

I answer by kissing him quickly and deeply and the whole room goes deathly quiet after that. I realize that it's the first time I've actually kissed one of the guys in front of the others. I freeze, scared to see the looks on Jensen and Tanner's faces. I finally do and it's interesting what I see. Tanner has a conflicted look on his face, not necessarily happy, but not angry either. Jensen's face just looks intrigued and a little hot...which is intriguing because Jensen is usually the possessive one in the group.

"So, I guess we're doing that now," says Jesse, the laugh in his voice rumbles against my chest. "It will be very rockstar of us," he jokes. When no one says anything, Jesse starts to walk towards the door with me still wrapped around him.

"Where are you going?" snaps Tanner as Jesse opens the door.

"It was my idea so I'm going first," Jesse says with a laugh and we leave before either of them can say anything. Once we're outside, he sets me down and we start to walk towards his truck holding hands.

"What do you want to do?" I ask once we're inside the truck.

"I have an idea," he says. He begins to drive, stopping by Starbucks to grab me my favorite coffee first so "I don't fall asleep on him."

My heart flutters when we drive until we get to the park where we first went to the music festival almost a year before.

We get out of the truck and Jesse surprises me by getting a blanket out of the truck. "I thought this idea just came to you?" I ask. He laughs.

"Ever since the concert I keep an extra blanket in my truck just in case I get the chance to recreate that day with you," he tells me, and I melt at his thoughtfulness. That day was one of the best days of my life, the day that I fell in love with him. I'm glad it meant something to him as well.

He walks to the exact spot we were at on that day and he spreads out the blanket. We both lay down on the blanket and stare up at the night sky. There's a tapestry of stars laid out before us and I have the sudden realization of how insignificant I am in the vast universe. It's a depressing thought.

I turn over on my side to look at Jesse. He shines like the stars. So talented, handsome, and full of life he's like a supernova exploding across the sky. I feel the heavy beat of love deep within me. It snuck inside when I first met him, and now I'm both helpless and powerful from its intensity.

Jesse turns over to look at me. "What are you thinking about, pretty girl?" he asks.

"Just how much I like you," I whisper. I'm too scared to put the other "l" word out there.

He leans towards me until we're only a heartbeat away from each other. Jesse sighs, a potent elixir against my lips. Pulling back just enough for his gaze to find mine, he strokes his fingers along my jaw. "I like you too, pretty girl. I think about you and me together so much I feel crazy. I am crazy. Fucking crazy for you." He kisses me, deep and long and still not enough. When he breaks away with a bursting breath, his eyes deepen into a sea blue.

He runs his hand up and fists them in my wavy mass, pulling it tight. "How do you do this to me? I'm completely out of control. Since I met you, every emotion I have is tied to how I think you're feeling. I've never felt like this in my life."

"Same here," I breathe and curl my other hand around his thick forearm. "I think … I think this is new for both of us." Jesse opens his eyes and looks at me for several long moments. Then he kisses me again, a long, but chaste kiss. Forehead to forehead, he whispers, "Say the word and I'll stay with you."

In that moment I want so much to take him up on his offer. I want to be selfish for the first time in my life and keep him, keep all of them. They are the first good thing that has ever been mine and I love them all so much. And because I love them, I know I can't keep them, at least for now.

"It's just a few months," I say, stroking the side of his face. I memorize his features like he always does to me.

"Promise me something," he says suddenly, his eyes flaring with intensity.

"Anything."

"Promise me that no matter what happens in the next few months, no matter what you hear or think you see, no matter what...that you'll get on that plane in four months and meet us in L.A."

There's not a doubt in my mind that I can keep this promise. I'll be there whether they want me there or not. "I promise," I tell him, sealing my vow with a kiss.

I stand up, suddenly desperate to give him something important to take with him while he's gone.

"Where are we going?" he asks as I pull him almost frantically to the truck.

"I need you to drive me to the warehouse," I tell him.

"If you want me to play something, we need to go back to the apartment. All that's left at the warehouse is an old piano since we packed everything up for L.A."

"Just take me there," I order him, and we drive to the warehouse without further argument. I'm shaking as he gets out the key and unlocks the warehouse door. I flip on the lights and turn to face him.

"I'm going to give you something right now that I've never given anyone," I tell him, kissing him softly on the lips and going to sit down on the piano bench. He silently comes to stand next to me.

Taking a deep breath for courage, I start to play the keys, just how I had been practicing in stolen moments in the music room during my study hall this year. Looking up at Jesse, I see his eyes widen when he sees that I can actually play. He gasps when he recognizes the Lady Gaga song that I've begun to play. I keep my eyes on his so that he can see how much this song is for him. I begin to sing for the first time in front of another person.

THAT ARIZONA SKY
    Burnin' in your eyes

You look at me and babe, I wanna catch on fire
It's buried in my soul
Like California gold
You found the light in me that I couldn't find

So WHEN I'M all choked up and I can't find the words
Every time we say goodbye, baby, it hurts
When the sun goes down
And the band won't play
I'll always remember us this way...

LONG AFTER THE last note fades, we sit there in the silence. I finally get the courage to look up at him and there's tears in his eyes. "Why have you been hiding this? I've never heard anything like that before," he says, his voice choked up with emotion.

"I just want you to remember this and take this memory with you. Remember us this way," I softly tell him. He kisses me. My lips to his, my life embedded with his, my tongue pressing inside for a taste that has to last us while he's across the country. I grab his wrists, digging my nails in and dragging them up his arms and around his shoulders, down his back until I hold on, holding him close as a sob crosses from my mouth to his.

When we're forehead to forehead, he grabs on to my gaze. "Please don't cry. Please don't. You're it for me, pretty girl." It's the closest he's come to I love you and I hold his words close to my heart.

The drive home is quiet. I stay at the apartment instead of going home thinking that I'll take advantage of every last second I have with them. I fall asleep between Jensen and

Tanner while Jesse sleeps on a mattress on the floor that he dragged into the room. It's a good thing I stayed there, because first thing in the morning someone from the label calls saying that they had to leave that day because a spot in the studio opened up early.

Our four-month separation turned into five years and I broke my promise to Jesse two weeks after they left.

I'd never met a boy like Tanner Crosby. He was a jumble of tattoos and muscle, a temptation for the good girl who never knew that she would want the bad boy with a wild abandon. I fell head over heels with a breathless sigh that first night I met him in a take me, marry me, give me a baby kind of way. It was like that with all of them. But in hindsight, Tanner was never really mine. He was a hurricane that materialized out of nowhere. All of the boys were. Being zipped into their whirlwind had been so crazy and unsteady and perfectly right all at the same time. Yet the first time I had heard them play I knew deep down as fast as they swept me off my feet, their storm would move on. And they wouldn't return.

Some sick feeling in the pit of my stomach had said so, but I'd listened to their promise that they would never leave me. And they hadn't left me. Not really. I had left them. I had loved them hard, and I didn't regret one minute. They had been my salvation. I'd never belonged anywhere or to anyone before them. I hadn't realized it, but when I moved to Bellmont, South Carolina I was desperate for something to shake up my life and save me. They had done everything they could, but I couldn't be saved.

I feel like I'm dying when I return backstage after the show and see Tanner walk into his dressing room with the red-headed girl from before the show.

I decide it's time to go home.

Jesse

I see her devastated expression as Tanner walks into his dressing room with Tanya. I know why he's taking her in there, and it has no connection with fucking...at least it doesn't anymore. I know Tanner well enough that once he saw Ariana, he wouldn't be able to even think about being with another girl, no matter how angry he is with her. Despite how upset I know Ari is about what she just saw, I'm not going to be the one to tell her the truth about who Tanner is now five years after she left us. Tanner can tell her himself. I've wasted enough time trying to save him.

I'm ashamed at how I acted right before the show. It's a physical struggle to not go over there right now and grab her and kiss her and love her and keep talking until she under-stands. Like I can force her to hear me or force her to love me. I've made so many mistakes, but it seems I just keep making them. Why did I tell her all of that? Of course she was going to freak out. Just hearing her reaction made me realize how dumb it was.

Without working too hard, I'd gotten what I wanted from women all my life. I traded on my looks and talent and then later my celebrity and got laid when I felt like it. That was the normal course of events. But of course, there's nothing normal about Ariana Kent. For five years I've been convincing myself that I did the right thing, that listening to Ari when she told us she was done with us and wouldn't be coming to L.A. was the right thing to do. I thought she just was going through a phase when she blocked our numbers and never answered our emails, that she would come to her senses eventually. But when weeks turned into months, and months turned into years, it became blaringly obvious that we had lost her.

The only thing I had left after that were memories and regrets. Why didn't I tell Ari that I loved her when I had the chance? I had known it the moment I had seen her in our History classroom. I know the truth of it. I was a coward. I'd already seen how much better she was than me, and I didn't want to love her and then risk her figuring that out … I didn't want to hear that Ari didn't want me. As I stare up at the white ceiling of the room and take a swig of my whiskey, I think about how I got to this moment where the girl I loved is the woman I barely know.

In my trip down memory lane I almost miss the fact that the woman in question is on her way out of the room. Desperation like I've never experienced courses through me. I can't let her go again.

ARIANA

"Ari!" Jesse snaps, before I can sneak out of the room. I freeze, unable to run away from the blatant longing and panic in his voice. "Where are you going?" he asks, grabbing my arm softly to turn me around to face him.

"I need to leave," I tell him. "I can't take anymore tonight."

"Stay with me tonight," he says, his eyes digging into my soul. I think of Gentry and how he actually hadn't called again tonight and how strange that was. I think of what will happen if Gentry finds out any of this. I think of the fact that Jesse needs to know that I'm unhappily married. And then I push all of those thoughts away and I decide that I'll take whatever consequences I get to spend one more night with Jesse. Everything else can wait until the morning.

"I'll drive and we can pick up your car in the morning," he tells me, and I nod. We walk out to a flashy red convertible that's a far cry from his black truck. He blushes when I tease him about it, and he explains that the car is a rental that the label picked out for him. I love that he's still enough of the old Jesse to be embarrassed about things. We drive out of the stadium backlot, listening to random songs on the radio and not really saying anything to each other.

I'm surprised when he pulls into the driveway of his old house, shifting the gear stick into park, and turning down the music. Sitting in one of our old make out spots I'm hit with a wave of longing. Longing to go back to the beginning with Jesse.

"I think the new owners of the house are probably going to have a problem with us sitting in their driveaway at midnight," I tell him, leaning back into the seat and absorbing how he looks in the moonlight streaming through the windshield.

"I bought the house after my parents decided to move. I guess some part of me just couldn't part with my memories here," he says.

"You bought the …" My words trail off as Jesse leans in towards me, his scent, his Jesse scent that I remember so well … sunshine … grass… clean, surrounds me. My pulse races. The car's headlights reflect off the white fence in front of us, slicing across his eyes, making them glow. A vibrant light blue, sucking me in. "Jesse—" Our air mingles. Mine are quick shallow breaths un-synched with my starving need for oxygen and reality.

"You think we're only back because of the tour, don't you?" he says quietly.

I lick my lips nervously, and nod. Jesse's eyes follow the movement.

"We begged," he whispered. "We pleaded, and we sold a little more of our soul to make it happen." His mouth tilts up into a grimace.

"I don't understand why you'd do that, Jesse."

"Yes, you do." He leans closer, and his arm comes up to brace on the driver's side door. "Seeing me whisper in that girl's ear tonight bothered you, didn't it?"

"No," I manage.

"Liar. Do you want to know what I was telling her?" I shook my head.

"No, definitely not."

The car suddenly goes still and silent as he turns the ignition off, then he shifts his body closer, sharing my air and not leaving enough for me. His hand goes around the steering column and flicks the headlights off. We are plunged into darkness. I swallow. It is a deafening sound. Every other sense goes into high alert. Closing my eyes, since there is no point in keeping them open, I feel his rough fingers skate up the column of my neck setting my nerve endings ablaze. His lips are close, close enough to taste again, if I just lean forward a little. I resist. My mouth waters.

Fingers dance over my cheekbone then slide behind my head pulling on my long locks of hair. Jesse inhales, breathing me in. "Ari," he murmurs. I know I should stop him, stop this, because my earlier behavior was already enough to damn me, but for a moment I just want to ... feel again. A thumb pad brushes down over the pulse beating wildly in my neck, and I let out a breath that hitches without my consent. I am thirsty for Jesse's mouth, but I refuse to close the miniscule distance.

"How can you tell me this isn't real?" Jesse whispers, his words caressing my mouth. Then his tongue flicks gently across my lower lip. Oh gosh. A small sound escapes me. I should have stopped him sooner.

"This is as real as it gets, Ari. This is Technicolor. Technicolor, when everything else is black and white. This …"

His hand trails down over the exposed skin of my chest then brushes over my top and the tip of my breast sending shock waves through me. I arch into his hand without meaning to. Damn my traitorous self. His hand doesn't stop, but floats down my belly to my thigh, and I tense, my mouth pressed tight to keep my reactions in, trembling on the edge of a place where my pride would cease to exist.

"This …" he continues and begins bunching up my skirt in his fist and drawing it up my thigh, "what we have … is extra-sensory overload … where everything else is a silent fucking movie." I pant out a breath then jam my jaw shut. My skirt glides up. Heat pools low in my belly. It is intoxicating. Would anything in my whole life ever feel this way? I'd been numb before they had first touched me and numb since they had been gone. I want to sob with the injustice of it. How could I still want to be consumed by them after all this time? I want to be inside on his bed underneath him. I want him to keep looking at me as if I'm his salvation. His benediction. His release.

But I know why I don't want it. I have nothing to give him in return. "This," I manage just as his hand releases my bunched-up skirt and lands hot on my bare upper thigh, sending waves of sensation cascading over my skin, "is just lust." Grabbing his face between my hands in the pitch dark, I close the distance and slant my mouth over his, sliding my tongue into his delicious mouth. Jesse groans deeply, and his fingers on my thigh dig in. He tastes so good. So … Jesse.

His face is hard and rough beneath my fingers, his mouth soft as he lets me in, kissing me back gently, not responding to my aggression. So, I kiss him harder, wanting to punish him for doing this to me. Wanting him to take over for me, make it so it wasn't my fault we were here. Make it so it was him kissing me. This was so messed up.

His gentleness and his refusal to respond to my fierce need do me in. And make me crazy. I pull my mouth from his, our erratic breathing reverberating around the interior of the vehicle. I struggle to shut down my body. He is heavy as I push at him in the pitch black, moving him away from me. Turning in my seat, I flick the car lights back on, and the light sloshes over the heated moment like ice water.

"I need you to take me back to my car, Jesse."

"What?" His voice is ragged, but I refuse to look at him. "Please. I can't do this with you. I won't. How can you even want to?" Jesse blows out a harsh breath and adjusts in his seat. Silence and unspoken words stretch out, winding their way around the car, sliding into all the available space between us and pressing me back into my seat with their weight. And then, I hear him move to start the car. He pauses as the interior light flickers on for a second, and the pressure between us releases.

"Tonight, that girl, like all of the girls, the interchangeable, available girls, that girl—offered to blow me."

I flinch and my stomach drops. "I don't want to hear this, Jesse. I'm very well aware of how busy all of you are kept."

"But I told her," he continues. "I told her that I had no intention of taking her up on her offer."

"Poor girl," I mutter sarcastically. He sighs and looks at me. His eyes are fierce, bitter, and vulnerable at the same time.

"I'm telling you about that girl to illustrate a point. I'm not just trying to get laid. I can get laid anytime I want. I'm a potential trophy fuck to pretty much every woman I meet."

There wasn't even a hint of arrogance in his expression, despite his words.

"Well done, Jesse. Very restrained. But seriously, while I appreciate you not rubbing my face in it because I was actually present in the room, what the hell does it matter?" I shrug my shoulders.

He gets out of the car suddenly and I hear rocks skittering away as he kicks at the ground, his back to me.

"Fuck!" he grinds out, and clutches both hands to his hair, grabbing fistfuls, his shoulder blades flexing under his t-shirt. He exhales loudly then turns back to me, his expression pained. "When this tour was approved, I decided I wanted to try and be good enough for you in the small chance there was that you even wanted me. I haven't slept with anyone in eight months."

"What?" My mind reels and my forehead creases in surprise and confusion. I know this is the moment I should tell him about Gentry, but I can't muster up the words with everything that he's telling me.

Jesse takes my hesitance as a negative. His jaw clamps down hard, and he takes a step back, before running a hand through his hair that's still damp from the shower he took after the show. My palms itch to do the same.

"I'm just going to say what I should have said five years ago when we were lying on that blanket under the stars at our park. There is nothing on this earth that I want more than you," he says, finally looking at me. "And from this moment on, I'm going to make sure you feel that every second of every day. You'll see it in my eyes when I look at you. You'll know, pretty girl, even when I'm gray, you're gorgeous, and we're rocking in chairs on our porch, that I love you. I fucking love you. And on the day I get down on one knee with a ring in my hand, when I beg you to be my wife because you're the best woman and the only one for me, you'll see love in my eyes."

He reaches up and roughly grabs two fistfuls of his hair before abandoning them in an unruly mess. "And you, Ari? What do you want?"

You, Tanner, and Jensen I think in my head. "I want … I want to be more than I am now," I say instead even though it's only partly the truth. I inhale deeply and then the words I've tried desperately to keep in spill out. "But, most of all, I don't want to have to keep living a life where you aren't in it."

He blinks, seemingly processing what I just said, storing it away, but I know what he heard was that I was saying yes. And I was. There was no way I was walking away from this. From him. From them. I couldn't deny it anymore, even if I couldn't figure out in the moment how I would get a divorce from Gentry.

Pursing my lips, I blow out a breath. I really hope I know what I just did. If we fail this time, it would break me irreparably. I reach my hands out slowly, hesitating before my fingertips make contact with his chest.

I can't wait anymore. I get out of the car and walk around to his side just as the sky decides to open and we begin to get soaked. We'd figure out the details later, and we'd do it together. I take a deep breath and press my palms against his now wet skin. Jesse's eyes close as he exhales and moves forward towards me. Sliding my hands around his ribs and up around his muscled shoulder-blades, I step into him. His arms curl around me, drawing me against him. One hand slides up into my hair and presses my face against his damp chest.

A barely controlled groan comes out with his next breath, reverberating against my skin. I revel in the feeling of his hot wet skin, his heart pounding beneath my cheek, my body pressed flush against his. So strong was the feeling of relief of being in Jesse's arms, it seems in that moment that nothing bad can ever happen to me ever again. The scent of his raw masculinity slides into my every pore, and my face turns to press my lips to his skin before I can question it. His body reacts beneath my touch. Bringing both hands to cup my face, he tilts it to look at him.

"I think this deserves a kiss," he rasps, staring at my mouth. I nod and moisten my lower lip in anticipation as he lowers his head. My pulse picks up a frantic beat as he closes in on me. I will myself to calm, but my breathing hitches as it gathers pace. I slide a hand up and around the back of his neck, tugging his mouth closer, because he was taking too damn long to get to me. The last thing I see is his dimple flash before his mouth meets mine.

This kiss is different than all the ones before, including at the stadium. We'd waited what seemed like forever for a kiss where there were no doubts between us. I open under him, meeting the slide of his tongue and moaning at the exquisite sensation. His lips are firm against mine, withdrawing and opening again, capturing my lips between his then sliding inside my mouth once more. I can taste the rain on them, and it only makes the kiss more perfect. Our heads shift and move, our mouths trying to find the perfect fit. The perfect rhythm. Trying to get closer, even though we are already drinking in each other.

Neither of us seem to want to stop and breathe more than the needy and necessary gasps that punctuate the moment. I grab a fistful of hair at the nape of his neck, and as his lips move over mine, I suck desperately at his bottom lip, grazing it with my teeth. My entire body is tuned to the kiss, focused on tasting him, the sweet mint on his tongue and the salt from his sweat, and every nip and pull of his mouth reach and pull sensation after sensation from the very depths of my body.

"Fuck," Jesse rasps against my mouth, pausing between thorough kisses. One of his hands leaves my face and wraps around my middle drawing me up and against him. Hard. "I realize you might want to move slower than our current pace..."

His fingers dig into me, pressing me closer. The hand at my face moves down my throat, tilting my head back, making room for his hot mouth as it leaves mine and slides to my chin then my ear, causing goosebumps to break out over my already sensitized skin. Slow? A giddy laugh bubbles up my throat, and I swallow unsure how to answer.

"You have to guide me here, pretty girl, or I ... shit," he says suddenly and lifts me off the ground. Swiveling around, he heads for the side door that leads into the kitchen. It's where I spent many an evening eating dinner with him and his family. As we walk in a thousand memories assail me. The house looks pristine despite the fact that it hasn't been inhabited for a few years.

"I pay a housekeeper to come in and keep it up," he explains, seeing the question in my eyes at the lack of dust on anything.

Still holding me, we ascend up the stairs and go into his bedroom. He sets me down in front of his bed that still has the same sky-blue comforter that I always thought matched his eyes. Standing there in front of the bed, I feel incredibly nervous. I'm no longer the innocent virgin I was when he knew me. I gave that up to Gentry on my wedding night, one of my biggest regrets considering how little he deserved that gift.

This feels like my first time again though just because they were always the one who I should have given it to. The gravity of the moment hits me and suddenly I can't do this with all these secrets between us. "Jesse, we need to talk. I have things I need to tell you," I whisper as he stands in front of me devouring me with his eyes as I stand in the moonlight streaming in from his window.

"I know there are five years' worth of life that we've both lived. And I know there's going to be hard conversations that we need to have. But I don't want to do that tonight," he says, lifting a hand to stroke my face. "I don't want anything from the past to change the future we are starting right now. No more thinking." He moves close, so close his nose brushes across the edge of mine. All I can feel is him. "Little by little, I'll prove this is real. When I'm done, you'll know this is about the beginning of you and me. You'll have a new truth."

"But I'm not . . ." His lips touch mine.

"Stop talking."

"Jesse." His mouth is on me. Touching.

"Ari." He kisses me. Pressing. Pressing hard.

He doesn't ask, he takes, nipping at my lips until they part and his tongue teases inside. The thick ridge of his growing erection digs against my stomach as he aligns his body with mine. Thoughts retreat as I get lost in him, in his kiss, his mouth and arms as they wind around my waist and haul me up so once again I freefall into Jesse's emotions. I give in. I mold to every rigid line of his body, my nails dragging down his shirt to feel his muscles ripple beneath my hands. My nipples pebble into hard knots, aching as they rub against cotton and his chest. Gosh. His fingers find my hair, tugging my head back to open my neck. He drags his teeth along my jaw and to my ear. "I love you." I groan, a lusty, wanton sound that brings his mouth back for a hard and demanding, totally mind-blowing follow-up kiss. My head spins. I'm going 'round and 'round on a roulette wheel.

Our clothes disappear in an instant and I don't even have a chance to admire his body before he's inside of me, crying out my name when our hips meet. I whimper and he pulls out all the way and slams back inside of me. I tremble as I rise to meet each thrust, every stroke, and it's my name that he chants. His name is on my tongue as he hovers above my mouth, taking in each grunted breath as I release it. And something happens. Something unlike anything I've experienced before, brighter than life, bigger than death, where lines between us blur, disappear, until we are new, born into one earth-shattering shape, whole and singular. Ari and Jesse don't exist, but we do. Us, just us. Together.

"More," I beg from beneath him.

"Give me everything," he whispers.

Everything. His control slips, and he rises above me, spreading my legs. Using my knees for leverage, he forces my thighs as far apart as they'll go, and seats himself inside. I shriek at the sensation. He sinks his fingers into my hips to hold me still as he rears back. He doesn't give me what I want though until my eyes meet his. He's beautiful.

"Jesse." He slams into me.

"You have me," he pants and then repeats. "All of me." I clutch him tight, holding him as close as possible and he fills me.

"Everything I have is yours. From here to eternity," he whispers into my mouth before he kisses me again.

I groan, and he kisses it away. He kisses me until I can't remember when I wasn't his, until my vision blurs and my lungs burn and so does my spine. The prickling ball of need pools at the base of my spine and spikes outward as I arch beneath him, fingers gripping the sheets and then his shoulders. I fall over the edge for the first time in my entire life, exploding into a fury of white light, giving him every last bit of me. Everything.

"Fuck, Ari," he moans as he feels me clench around him. He plants his nose next to my ear, as if he's inhaling me. The smell of sex and forever drives him forward, driving through my orgasm while he chases his own one snapping thrust at a time until he follows me into bliss. Time ticks to the beat of our twitching muscles and panted breath. He's crushing me with his weight, but I can't bear to be apart from him. He begins to move off of me. "Don't go, please," I whisper.

"I'm not going anywhere, pretty girl," he says while licking down my neck. "That was so much better than anything I ever imagined. I like everything about being right here with you. You okay with a sleepless night? Because I'm not nearly done with you. I'll never be done with you."

We lay there entwined and as I think about the last twenty-four hours and everything that has happened, I start to cry. I just had the most beautiful experience of my life and I haven't told him about Gentry. And what does it say about me that lying entwined with him I'm wishing Jensen and Tanner were here at the same time.

He kisses the tears as they fall down my face. "Ari, what's wrong? Did I go too hard? Did I hurt you?"

"No, no," I rush to assure him, burrowing my face in his neck. "It's just...I feel terrible, because I love you so much, more than anything." I say. "And that was the best moment of my entire life. But I still miss them," I tell him, and I begin to sob harder.

"Pretty girl," he says softly, lifting off of me and rolling beside me so that we can look at each other. "I know you love them too, that you've always loved them. We would talk about it all the time back then, about what we would do if you ever picked. I know that they love you just as much as I do, and we'll figure it out."

I look at him shocked. "You're okay with that?" I ask him in awe.

"Being theirs doesn't make you any less mine," he tells me with a smile. "Especially when I get you like this because I'm the least idiotic out of all of us and took advantage of you being back the fastest."

I laugh at how proud he is. "They hate me," I tell him.

"They don't hate you. They just have more demons than I do. Just give them time." A look of vulnerability passes over him. "You're going to stay with us, right? You're finally ours?"

I think of Gentry and how insurmountable it seems to escape him. But I'll do it. I'll do anything not to lose this.

"I'm yours," I whisper. We drift off to sleep in his childhood bedroom, and I never sleep better.

12

I wake up alone, and I don't like it. I have a momentary
freak-out that he left, but then I hear pots and pans
banging from downstairs, followed by a muttered curse,
and I calm down. I get out of bed and slip my panties and bra
back on along with his t-shirt that he left up here. My phone
falls out of my clothing when I pick it up and I feel the flash of
panic I always get when it comes to anything related to Gentry.
I'm filled with dread as I look to see what calls I missed.
There's none. The dread intensifies just because Gentry never
has gone a few hours without calling me when he's out of
town let alone almost an entire day. He even calls me multiple
times during the night just to make sure I'm there. One time he
called me while he was in bed with his fuck of the night. I feel
like he's playing some kind of sick game with me, and I'm not
sure what to do.

Finally deciding that I just need to wait until he calls and
deal with everything then, I walk out of the room and down
the stairs. I stop before I get to the bottom to admire him for a
second as he cooks something over the stove in the kitchen, a
tower of maleness and hard muscle.

He turns around when the last stair squeaks as I step on it. A smile spreads across his stubbled jaw when he sees me. "Morning, pretty girl," he says.

"Hi," I mumble, feeling shy all of a sudden standing in front of him in just his shirt. I cross my arms over the shirt, hoping he won't notice my breasts. They're suddenly achy, and the pang is enough to force heat to burst on my cheeks.

"You're up early," he says to me, looking out the window that's just beginning to show the markings of a new day.

"So are you. I thought rockstars were supposed to party all night and sleep all day?" I ask jokingly, heading to the counter and the coffee that I hope is waiting for me somewhere.

"I've never fit the mold on that. You know I've always loved mornings," he says with a smile, gesturing for me to sit at one of the bar stools at the counter. My insides feel fluttery when I see the tender look that he's giving me. It's been a really long time since someone waited on me. If he wants to wait on me, I'll accept.

With his back to me, Jesse pulls out two cups and pours what he already has brewed. I train my vision on admiring the beautiful kitchen; it's much more G-rated than the rockstar covered in black ink ending above a very tight ass.

"How do you like it?" he says holding up the mug, and I get stuck on his voice. It's thick molasses this morning, and it sinks in and tingles all the way to my toes.

"The same way as I did," I whisper, and I feel a pang of regret at the relief that flashes briefly in his eyes. It's not as hard to forget all the years that have passed now that it's morning.

He grabs my cup and puts one spoonful of sugar and a dash of milk in it and hands it over to me. I immediately take a sip, thinking it somehow tastes better than usual just because he made it. After watching me take a sip in what looks like a trance, he shakes his head briefly and then goes to the stove and grabs a pan from it that's filled with eggs. He spoons out the eggs on two plates and slides one over to me.

"Eat," he orders, and my eyes shoot up at his command. He holds my gaze and slides the eggs and then some toast he grabs from the toaster further in front of me.

"You're bossy," I say, but pick up my fork anyway. Like the coffee, breakfast is delicious. He watches me eat for a moment.

"You look too skinny," he says softly and my fork freezes mid-air before I go back to eating like I didn't hear his comment. He leans over across the counter just then, a concerned look in his eyes. He walks around brushing my hair behind me.

"What the fuck is this, Ari," he asks, gesturing to where I realize there are probably handprint sized bruises on my neck that I haven't kept hidden this morning.

"Who the fuck did this to you?" he asks, his face contorted with rage and pain.

"A monster," I tell him.

"I'll kill him," he replies fiercely.

"He's never going to be a problem again," I tell him, although I know even as the words come out that they are a lie.

He tips up my chin. "Pretty girl," he whispers. "You think you don't deserve to share yourself, your secrets. You think you burden people with your darkness. But you don't. You're not dark. You're light. You're warmth. You're good. Fuck. Ari," his voice broke, "you are so good." My entire body trembles, a need to hold him wars against my stubbornness. And yet, I can't believe the words he is saying.

How could he believe I wasn't dark? If your soul was comprised partly from experience, then my soul would at the very least be some shade of grey. And each lie I told hung heavy on the dark side, slipping the gradient scale more towards the dark. I didn't believe light and dark could exist without the other. It was the absence of light that made us dark in the first place. And while I wasn't wallowing in some emotional self-pity, I knew my soul was more dark than light. I was more bad than good. And it was with that realization that had made me make my original choice to walk away from them all. Not because I was dark, but because they were not.

"I'll make you believe it," he says fiercely, and I want to believe him.

"Ok, I have an idea," he says grabbing me suddenly and twirling me around until I laugh. "Assuming you don't have any plans today you can come back with me to the stadium and hang out while we get ready for the show tonight and then you can sit through another of our boring ass concerts," he says with a wink. "Then we can figure everything out after that."

I'm nervous to see Tanner and Jensen again after the disaster of last night, but I also feel desperate to see them at the same time.

"Okay," I tell him, knowing that I would follow him anywhere.

My emotions are all over the place as we pull into the stadium parking lot. I wait for Jesse to open the door for me and for a second, it's like we're in high school again. He takes my hand as we walk into the stadium and I'm still not sure how this is my life all of a sudden.

We walk into the green room and I want to leave as soon as we do since Tanner and Jensen are screaming at each other. They stop as soon as they see us. Jensen gives me a dirty look.

"What the fuck is she doing here?" he asks before stomping away into a back room.

"He just needs some time," Jesse says gently, and I nod like I agree with the idea.

Some time. I don't know if there is enough of it in the world to conquer this mountain. My heart plummets to my stomach, and the room is suddenly too small. With Jesse's sympathetic eyes watching me, I retreat, mumbling something about needing to make a call as I rush out of the room. I hurry to the room where Tanner had kissed me the night before. Just as I turn to shut my door, Tanner's arm sneaks in, and then his chest and the painful sigh he lets out as he enters. Tanner looks exhausted. His eyes are red-rimmed, his hair is all over the place. He doesn't look like he's slept at all. I immediately want to take care of him but I'm not sure that he would welcome that.

"Princess." One word. One word and I crack. I step forward, a tactical error on my part. He grabs my wrist, tugging me into his arms and holding me impossibly still with his powerful grip to my waist. His gaze burns into me, fierce and determined. Before I can say his name, my hands are pinned to his chest and his mouth slams down on mine. He takes in my cry, using his tongue to tame me. I squirm against his brute strength, straining on his lap when he falls into a chair. My resistance only wedges my ass on his lap.

Frustration bubbles up, and I bite his lip, thinking of the girl from last night. He groans and so I do it again, harder this time, but he squeezes my aching breasts in retaliation. Holy crap. I break away, gasping and arching in a lust that's painful in its severity. This is pure torture. Just like Tanner Crosby.

"Ari," he breathes out my name as his fingers begin to trail up my neck away from where I want him to go. Oh, gosh. I wrestle away, but he holds me in place with his free hand, all the while continuing his slow seduction of my body. "I didn't sleep with that girl. I drank too much and yes, Tanya was there too, but nothing happened. Nothing. Look at me."

I don't want to. The white ceiling is fascinating.

"Look at me," he says in the tone that has always commanded my attention. When that doesn't work, he tweaks my nipple, and I almost come off his lap like a rocket. My eyes find his in shock. "I fucked up. I know it as well as you. But I didn't do anything we can't recover from."

"Tanner, you don't owe me anything. You can do whatever you want. You haven't been mine for a very long time."

"We both know that's not true. I was back to being hopelessly wrapped around your finger the second you appeared in the doorway yesterday," he says almost bitterly.

I forget that I hate hope. It prickles at the back of my mind and opens my heart like a budding flower. He must sense my vulnerability. In a second, he slips his fingers into my hair and pulls me in for another kiss that's so full of longing and desire that I feel like I could die. My body flushes with need. I need him.

"Princess?"

I groan, hating how much this all hurts. It's much worse than anything I could have imagined.

"Tanner?" I finally answer.

"I need to tell you something important. Will you let me?"

I cringe, taken back to the days when I had said almost those exact words to them on the phone when I let them go. Tears blur my vision, and squeezing my lids closed in a hard blink does little to clear it. "Go ahead," I mumble.

"My truth is not an excuse—it just is. My head is full of noise, and it's gotten worse. It's been really bad lately. And I'm mixed up with some stuff. And then seeing you yesterday…."

He swallows.

"What does that mean?" I ask, afraid to know. Pain pinches his features together and a quick breath unravels the hurt leaving him open and exposed. He sighs and looks away from me and I immediately know the answer.

Drugs.

His admission sucks the air from my lungs. After years of wondering if the reports are true, I've just found out that they are. And he used them last night. Guilt prickles at my nape. I should have stayed at the stadium and gone after him even if he was with Tanya, yet I let my pride and insecurities shut me down.

"How bad is it?" I ask, my heart clenching painfully as I wait for an answer.

"I've been using a lot more lately, some harder stuff too, but I'm going to stop. I can stop whenever I want," he says, looking at the ceiling and then back at me, pleading with his eyes for me to believe him. I remember another time when he said almost those exact same words to me.

"Do you need to get some help?" I ask carefully.

"I've been to rehab a few times. I'm sure you saw the rumors in the news. But I only went because the Label made me. I'm fine. I only do it when I'm stressed, but it's going to stop," he says again. His hands tangle in my hair until I feel like I'm getting some kind of sensual head massage. "I need you to believe me when I say I'm in this however you want me. I want us. I want this, everything that comes along with you. I won't hurt you."

Some of the tension holding my stiff spine eases, and I relax against him. But not all of it. I grab the back of his shoulders to set myself upright to watch his reaction.

"Did *anything* happen with Tanya last night?" I ask.

"No."

"Did you want to?"

"No." His brow pulls down in a twisted knot of confusion. "Tanya's been my supplier for years and I guess ya, I've been fucking her lately. But she's nothing. I wouldn't be able to even get it up for her after seeing you again," he says.

As he says his piece, his hand resumes its incessant rubbing and he smiles. "But I can't stop thinking about you. I didn't sleep all night because I kept going over that kiss and thinking about kissing you everywhere. I've thought about you constantly for five years. Do you remember the very first time we met?"

My heart thrums too fast because I do.

"I owe you the truth, Ari. I'm ready to give it to you. Please."

Please. As if I can say no. I nod, and he continues on a rushed breath, "I've been in love with you since I saw you that night. At first, I tried to talk myself out of the feelings, I knew I wasn't any good for you. But I've dreamed about you every night since I've met you and all I've ever been able to think was mine. Mine, Ari. Just mine. The word bounces like a pinball in my head and my heart every time I hear your name. I've never stopped wanting you."

He sucks in a breath and shudders. "But I broke a promise to you. I told you that last day that I would come for you no matter what. But I was so angry with you, for what you said during that call. I should have come after you. I'm an idiot, Princess, but I always see you. It's impossible not to. I've made more mistakes than I'd like to admit. Getting high last night and making you think I was with another girl was one of them. Life crashed in on me seeing you again and I shut down, shut off everything. Please forgive me," he murmurs, drawing out my grief through tears I had yet to cry.

He kisses me everywhere—cheeks, chin, forehead, and down to my ear, mixing his sadness with my own. A storm surges up and out of my chest, angry and consuming. This is my fault, not his. I pound Tanner's chest, wrestle his shirt into my fist and let him hold my sagging frame. And he does, so tight I have nowhere to go. We weep through his guilt, my guilt, the years we've lost, and into the forgiveness he so desperately thinks he needs.

Tanner finds my eyes, never breaking contact as he bends with his lips hovering over mine. Hard and desperate, his gaze penetrates through my grief and into something new. I shift in his arms and the slightest movement alters our axis. His lids flare for a moment, and then he presses his mouth to my own again. Is it possible for something to be right and wrong at the same time? This...this feels so good. Like unspoken words expressed in a rush of breath and weighted meaning. I know him. I know his thoughts and fears, and I pull him impossibly closer to soothe his ache and to ease mine. His tongue slips between my lips and he's fierce, demanding as he licks and bites into me until I'm drunk on feeling. I match his movements, his groan, the tug of hands in hair. Our hearts break and with the same emotion that destroyed us, we pick each other up and rebuild.

Everything changes.

The darkness behind my eyes brightens as I squeeze my lids together just to feel him pressed tightly to my aching breasts. A mimicked pant escapes in a burst when he withdraws just enough to drag in air. We're consumed and possessed. The world narrows to two bodies longing for more than this night will bring. Tanner is greedy, but he gives as much as he takes. I like kissing him, a lot. Too much for it to continue, so I press against his shoulders. Then I groan and curse as a knock sounds on the door. He breaks away, dazed. A second passes as we stare at one another before someone pounds on the door again.

"You're on in five," says one of the crew, and Tanner takes a step away. His hands are clenched into tight fists, and his breathing is coming out labored.

"I have to go," he says roughly, and I want to cry. It's only the unspoken things that sifts between us that tells me everything will be alright.

Jensen

As we perform, I stare at the woman who has tormented my dreams and every waking moment for the past five years. I can't believe she's actually standing in front of me. Living, breathing, alive. Jesse and Tanner fought for this stop for months while this tour was being planned, hoping that if we came, somehow she would appear. But I hadn't wanted it despite the fact that every day without her felt like torture. She had broken my heart into a thousand pieces. Taken my love and thrown it away like it was nothing. My feelings for her were torturous in their intensity. They weren't love, because the feelings weren't light or happy. They were dark and weighed heavily on my heart. She was a poisonous addiction that I hadn't been able to kick. I wouldn't give in this time.

13

ARIANA

If I have been one thing in life, it's someone's responsibility. I started off as an obligation to parents who never wanted children. An abortion wasn't an option by the time my mother confirmed her pregnancy, a detail she was never above mentioning. Then, the boys had taken care of me when I moved to Bellmont, protecting me and sheltering me from my dark world. Gentry, in his sick way, had taken responsibility for me over the last few years. But it all ended tonight. The last thing I'll ever be to anyone again is a duty, a mission, a task for completion. I can't move on with Jesse and Tanner...and hopefully Jensen, with Gentry looming in the background. It has to end. I'm not sure how it's going to happen, but I'll do anything to make sure it does.

I sneak backstage before the show finishes, and I leave a note for the guys with their assistant Emily saying that I have to take care of something and that I'll meet Jesse back at his house as soon as it's done. Scared but resolute, I walk to my car and drive for the last time to the hell hole that I've been kept prisoner in.

The house is quiet and dark when I walk in. Every part of

me aches to be back with them but I know that in order to start over I have to somehow find a way to fix the biggest mistake I've ever made. Gentry will be home in the morning, and I'll have my bags packed.

"Forget something?" comes Gentry's cool voice from within the dark cave of the living room. I squint and can see him sitting in his lazy boy rocker, a bottle of something dangling from his hand.

"Gentry," I say, in a quiet, resigned way as I walk towards him. Icy-cold fear sinks into my veins as I stand there staring at him for one stunned second. He looks terrible, nothing like he looked before he left just the day before. His blond hair is stringy, his light eyes wide and crazed. He's unshaved and it looks like he slept in his clothes. Worse, he radiates a dark cruelty, the cold fury he possesses unable to be ignored. Staring at him I can't help but think how repulsive I think he is, like a clay version of a human being. If I cut him open, insects and maggots would probably spill out instead of blood.

He doesn't just appear malicious; he seems unstable in a way he hasn't before, as if he's lost whatever was holding him in check before. I force my lungs to suck in air and my brain to start working. It finally hits me that I'm probably in a lot of danger since he's home a whole day early. I look wildly behind me, somehow hoping that anyone will be right outside of the still open front door. Gentry stands up suddenly and I gasp as he stalks towards me. He reaches out and grabs my arms.

"Aren't you happy to see me?" he growls at me, his eyes narrowing menacingly. "Cause it's not looking that way...wife. I saw you leave the house yesterday and I know you haven't been home since then. Who have you been fucking? I can smell it all over you. You swore you'd love, honor, and obey me. I'm here to make sure you keep that promise."

"You're home early," I whisper lamely, my eyes darting

around the room for something, anything, I can use to defend myself if it comes down to it. I straighten my back and glare at Gentry, wondering how I had managed to put up with this sad, pathetic man for five years. "I'm leaving, and if you do anything, I have people that know where I am, and they will come for me. Even you won't be able to escape jail after that," I say, even though it's a lie.

"No, I don't think you're going anywhere," says Gentry with an evil smile. Gentry lifts up his shirt, forcing me to look down against my will. My stomach lurches when I see the glint of a blade and the grim smile of promise on his face.

"Remember saying 'till death do us part'? One way or the other, you're keeping those vows, Ariana, and it doesn't make a difference to me which one. I have no problem killing you and leaving you for your lover to find. So, go ahead and scream; maybe you two can die together."

I look around the house, feeling trapped in one of those horrible news stories. I could already see the headlines: ex-husband stabs wife in a jealous rage. Hadn't we been heading this direction for years?

"How did you know I had left the house?" I ask quietly, my eyes on the gun he's now holding in his hand.

"I know you, Ariana. I know everything about you because you're mine. You started acting strange the second my bitch of a mother mentioned that concert. I knew you would go and try to see them play. It's pathetically hilarious how I was able to put up cameras to watch you without you knowing."

I look at him shocked, but he continues before I can say anything.

"You think I didn't do my homework on you when we met, that I didn't hear all the stories of how you were once the band slut and then they had left you?" He laughs cruelly. "I knew you would go to that concert, but I didn't know that you would fuck a stranger while you were there."

I realize with a sense of relief that he doesn't know that I've been with the band. He thinks I just hooked up with a random person at the concert. I need to keep him thinking that as long as possible, so he doesn't do anything to go after them.

Suddenly he lunges at me. Vodka. Scent was the strongest sense tied to memory and I believed it in this moment as memories flashed of all the times I'd smelled that smell. And it was then that I felt fear, true, bone-chilling fear. This man abused me for years and now he wants me dead. The memories instantly weaken me, and he easily overpowers me. The next thing I know, I am flat on my back on the floor. Gentry climbs over me, one hand on my mouth and the other clamping my wrists together. His weight presses me into the wood. His hand on my mouth. My stomach clenches, readying to purge its contents as a memory tries to break through again. I twist my head, back and forth, trying to bite.

The hand over my mouth moves away, but before I can do anything, that hand moves to my throat, squeezing hard enough to crush. I start panicking, my thoughts aren't clear. My wrists are trapped tightly, and my air is being choked off. I can't think about anyone or anything. I knew each second was bringing me closer to unconsciousness and I was helpless to stop it.

And then, an image flashes across my mind of a starry sky. Jesse, I think. My brain kick-starts, surging one last burst of energy through my body. I twist my hands in Gentry's grasp at the same time as I bring my knee up between his legs again. He grunts and shifts his weight, freeing my legs which I use to start thrashing, shifting him further off of me. I gasp when his hand finally leaves my throat. He's still over me though, breathing on me.

I lift my head hard enough to hit his. My head instantly registers the ache at the crack of our skulls, but he lets go of my hands which I use to deliver repeated hits to his face. Tears burn paths down my face, but I push harder, hit harder, until I'm able to push his weight off of me completely. I roll away to my feet but my ankle collapses, so I drag myself against the wall and slump back against it as he pulls himself to his knees in front of me. I'm shaking now, my entire body feels the effects of exhaustion. I grip the railing in my hands and lift my leg to hit him, but he intercepts, grabbing my ankle and wrenching it. I scream, a silent, choked sob. Fire rips through my body, burning a path up and down my leg. The tears come harder and my throat aches to release the cry that chokes my breath. I was at his mercy, with my ankle in his hand. And he knew it. He wrenches it harder and my body is overcome with shakes. I hear the flick of a knife. No, no no. It wasn't until that moment that I realize my own mortality. I lunge, reaching for the knife in his hand, eventually knocking it from his grasp. I hear it skid across the wood planks of the floor and I dive for it. My ankle is completely useless. I pull myself up to lean once again against the wall, the knife in hand, trying to catch my breath.

He lunges for me again, sending us both into the wall, shattering the dry wall. I lose the knife upon impact. Gentry recovers more quickly than I do, wrapping a hand around my loose hair and pulling me tightly to him. I yank my head, finally feeling my body come to life again. I try to free my hair from his grasp.

"You're mine," he says hoarsely. He's distracted for a moment as he talks and I grab the lamp on the table next to us and slam it against his head, sending him sprawling to the ground. I take the chord and stretch it across his throat. He starts to panic and thrash against me, but I hold on. Right before he looks like he's going to pass out, I let up and he sucks in a huge breath, the mottled blue of his face slowly fading. There are angry red welts on his throat from the cord. He stares at me with an animalistic obsession burning out of his eyes. He lays on the ground keeping his eyes on me warily since I'm still holding the lamp in my hands.

Gentry was a perpetual victim, scurrying to fill the emptiness of his soul, and sucking the life out of those around him for his fuel. I itched to find the knife and stab him again and again, for all he'd done to me, but I know in that instant, it wouldn't really make a difference. I would be the only one who would be punished. I couldn't kill him. Hopefully me finally being able to stand up to him would prevent him from following me into my new future.

"You're my wife and you'll always be my wife," he croaks out, shattering that last thought. I clench my fist at those hideous words.

I suddenly swing the lamp at his head. He's unable to move in time since he's still recovering from almost choking to death. The base of the lamp shatters on his head and he goes unconscious, blood drizzling from a large gash in his forehead. He's still breathing, but he will be out for a while. Long enough for me to leave without interference.

"Not anymore," I whisper to his still body. And then I limp out of the room.

14

The drive to Jesse's house seems to take forever. I left my car and called an Uber since I didn't want Gentry to be able to accuse me of taking anything that wasn't mine. He was still breathing when I left, so I'm almost positive that he will live. And then he'll come for me. But I won't think about that now.

Jesse

I've been sitting and waiting in the house all night in hopes that she would return. She had promised she would in the note, but the memory was still fresh in my mind of another time that she promised she would meet us and never did. I finally can't stay still anymore, and I start pacing. If she doesn't come by dawn I am going to go try to find her. Surely someone in this town will know where she lives. It's amazing thinking about it, how Ariana has in two days destroyed me with anger, held me while I wept like a baby, and built me back up with the promise of her love. She thinks that I need to pick up all of her pieces, but all I can think about is putting her back together with my soul wrapped around hers.

I'm a second away from getting in my car to go find her when the door behind me opens. I turn, just as the sun breaks in through the window behind me as it rises. Ariana limps in, a tremulous smile on her face. She's still here, all of her, and she's somehow more. Taller somehow. The colors around her glow brighter and hell, I love her. I have never loved anything so much in my life as I love Ariana in the moment she steps out of the shadows and into the sun.

ARIANA

The afternoon sun falls across my face much earlier than I would like from the window we forgot to pull the curtain over. Jesse turns me to face him, hands on my shoulders. His gold hair is messy, like he'd been tugging on it or sleeping under a pillow. My fingers itch to slide through the glossy locks and pull his rugged face and full lips down to mine. I've had his body all morning and I still want more. His eyes roam my face, and he must have the same thought, because we both move into each other, our lips meeting, the relief of touching him gliding through me in a ripple of longing.

"Hi," I manage through kisses.

"I missed you," he breathes. "Even when I'm sleeping, I miss you."

I sigh. Having Jesse this close again is like having dessert over and over. Decadent and sweet. I press a kiss to his chest.

"You're sweet when you wake up," I tell him with a giggle at his sappiness.

"Don't get used to it," Jesse says against my ear. "This is

just the honeymoon period. Tomorrow I'll kick your ass out of bed for some coffee."

I laugh. I had forgotten how much I laughed around Jesse. The laughter reminds me how much my throat and my ankle still hurt from what Gentry did to me last night. It's time to tell Jesse everything.

"We need to have our talk now," I tell Jesse, watching as he nods, and his eyes change to the color of a churning surf in turquoise waters at the seriousness in my voice.

I feel something turn over in my chest when our eyes connect. I'd said before that he looked at me like he wanted to reach inside of me, open me up. But he already has. He's seen the darkness and he's stayed. He's found me.

As I open my mouth to start telling my story, we hear the front door open, and footsteps sounding down the hall. Our door bursts open right as I'm pulling the covers up over my body. Tanner and Jensen storm in. They stop short when they see us, a mix of hate, envy, and longing present in their faces that is difficult to interpret.

Jesse moves his body in front of me, blocking their view. His protectiveness sends a burst of love through my heart. I melt into the back of him, peeking over his shoulder at the two men who hold the rest of my heart in their hands. Any happiness I've been feeling freezes at Jensen's next words.

"Did she tell you she was married before you fucked her?"

CONTINUED **in Remember You This Way...**
Books2read.com/rememberyouthisway

REMEMBER YOU THIS WAY

Continue the journey withe the Sound of Us in Remember You
This Way…out now! Books2read.com/rememberyouthisway

AUTHOR'S NOTE

I've been in love with rockstar romances since I first knew they existed. I think I've read every book that Goodreads has ever suggested on the subject. That being said, this book just gutted me to write. I love these characters. I love their pasts, their presents, and their futures, and I have so much planned for them in this trilogy.

Now, I know what you're thinking. There C.R. goes again with her cliffhangers, but #sorrynotsorry. This one was so needed! I know you have questions like what happened to Ariana that prevented her from going to L.A., where did the scars come from on Tanner's back, what is Jensen's past? Are there going to be more scenes with Tanner and Jensen? Fear not, I considered this book "Jesse's" book and each guy will get their own book that is focused on them. All will be revealed my darling readers...and the series is complete, so just keep on reading!

Thank you as always for embarking on this journey with me. Please leave a review on Amazon to give me further motivation to keep the story going. As I've said before, I read all of my reviews and I'm grateful for anyone that takes the time to tell me what they think of Ariana's story.

P.S. Read on after this page to get the first chapters of my dark mafia romance, Ruining Dahlia!

Visit my **Facebook** page to get updates.

Visit my **Amazon Author** page.

Visit my **Website**.

Sign up for my **newsletter** to stay updated on new releases, find out random facts about me, and get access to exclusive scenes from books.

SNEAK PREVIEW

Here's a preview of my standalone dark mafia book, Ruining Dahlia. Available on Amazon and KU at books2read.com/ruiningdahlia.

RUINING DAHLIA

I was sold to my enemies. **And not just my enemies.** *I was sold to monsters.*

I should know all about how to survive monsters though, I come from a family of them. We aren't Butchers in name only, after all.

I'm shipped away to New York City to the powerful head of the Costa Nostra, the Rossi Family.

My first meeting with them is bloody and wild, just like they are.

Lucian, Raphael, and Gabriel Rossi...they own me now. And they won't let me forget it.

A dahlia has always bloomed best in the light, but they're determined to keep me in the dark.

The thing they don't realize is that I'm more than what I seem. It's a race to the ending, me against them.

They want to ruin me. And I'm afraid I just might like it.

CHAPTER 1

DAHLIA

I t was dark.

Isn't that how all these tales go?

Maybe everything had always been dark for me though, since the moment I took my first breath as a baby. Always somber. Always sad.

An ache inside of me that the doctors and the medicine could never fix.

I laid in bed that night, listening to the sounds of the party that my parents were throwing to celebrate some deal that The Firm had managed to enter into.

There was a nightlight across the room, its light a beacon that I would stare at every night until finally I drifted off to sleep.

I had always been scared of the dark. Which was a strange thing in itself since I just confessed to living in it.

But ever since I could remember, I'd needed a light on.

At first, I'd been allowed to have the closet light on, but then my father had insisted that "no child of his was going to be afraid of the dark," and from that moment on, it wasn't allowed. He'd gone so far as to unscrew my lightbulb at night so I could "get over my fears." It was only my continual screaming at night that got him to allow me a small nightlight. When I was away at school, I always kept the light on in my room, but here I was, back home on holiday, the nightlight my only saving grace.

A small creak sounded in the room. I flinched at the noise, my eyes desperately searching the darkness to see what monster was waiting in the dark corners of my room. I watched in terror as the door to my closet inched open, the sound of its creaking scraping down my spine, and a massive form stepped out from its depths.

I opened my mouth to scream, just praying that the music wasn't too loud and that someone would be able to hear me before it was too late.

"It's just me, pet," my uncle's voice whispered in the darkness.

I trembled beneath my blankets, sliding farther away from him until I hit the wall, because I knew even at eight there was no good reason for my uncle to be hiding in my closet.

His footsteps were soft as he ambled towards me, his features becoming clear as he walked into the nightlight's purvey.

"Please get out," I hoarsely begged, not sure what to do. My Uncle Robert was my father's right hand. A skilled killer whose name was synonymous with The Firm.

My father would never believe me over him.

"Don't be afraid, Dahlia," he whispered as he reached my bed.

I whimpered and pulled the covers up closer to my chin.

I cried when he slid into the bed with me, his hands traveling over my skin.

I shattered into a million pieces when he first stroked his finger across my knickers. The darkness that lived inside me spread through my veins, until any light that had been trying to survive was extinguished, leaving me an empty husk.

But I didn't cry after that.

Or the time after that.

Or the time after that.

I didn't cry ever again.

TWELVE YEARS Later

"Bollocks," I murmured as a busy passerby shoulder-swiped me as they walked past, the white chocolate mocha in my hand going flying all over the pristine white blouse that I'd mistakenly chosen for this flight. For some inane reason, I'd thought that getting all dressed up before my eight-hour flight made sense.

Not that the man waiting for me at the end of the flight would care if I was dressed up or not. He probably wouldn't care if I showed up in a paper bag...or if I showed up at all.

Butterflies swarmed inside me just thinking of what lay ahead. I'd stopped in the middle of the walkway to assess the damage, so it wasn't a surprise when someone knocked into me again, spilling the rest of my drink.

"Fuck," I griped as I finally did the sensible thing and scurried out of the way of the thousands of people milling around in the Heathrow airport today. I'd never been in a public airport before. I'd always been on a private plane courtesy of the wealth of my father, Trevor Butcher. But he was gone now, and my brother...along with my new fiancé had apparently thought that commercial was the way to go.

For a moment, I imagined melding into the crowd and

setting off for some exotic locale to be lost in. I imagined golden beaches, and drinks with the little umbrellas in them… or maybe an idyllic lake setting where I'd spend my days on a dock, watching wisteria grow over my bare feet, writing the next great novel which would never see the light of day.

I would have thought them all foolish to send me on my own. A girl even an ounce braver than me would be running for the hills, desperate not to marry a perfect stranger. After all, they didn't know the nightmares that waited for me here in England were far worse than anything I could comprehend waiting for me in New York. They didn't know how close I'd been to trying to get away…permanently.

Or maybe they did. My stomach clenched at the thought. Maybe they saw the ruin in me. Either way, my warped, damaged self somehow held some loyalty to "The Firm"…so here I was, the obedient daughter to the very end.

I shook my head, trying to push away the memories and images that seemed to be permanently etched into my mind.

That was all behind me now. This was my fresh start. I threw my now empty cup away and looked around to see if there were any airport shops I could get a new shirt from, since my bags and belongings were all either checked already or shipped to New York ahead of me. I wandered through the airport, glancing at the stores, searching for anything that might sell clothing, until I stopped and turned around, not wanting to get too far from my gate.

See…the perpetual good girl to a fault.

I weighed my options as I spotted a shirt sporting the Union Jack in one of the gift shops. Which was worse, meeting my future husband with a brown stain that resembled shit all over my shirt…or wearing that?

Union Jack it was.

My hand reached for the shirt at the same time another

hand did, and our skin brushed against each other, until I yanked my hand away like I'd been burned.

I turned my head to apologize, but my words got lost at the blond Adonis standing next to me.

Everyone was looking at him. It was impossible not to. He was beautiful. Like Chris Hemsworth and Henry Cavill had merged into one being and then been touched by Midas.

And that description wasn't an exaggeration.

It was his eyes that caught me first. They were the color of a thousand dancing waves, the exact color of pictures I'd seen showing the Caribbean. Or maybe not the Caribbean. They seemed to change the longer I stared. Maybe they were more like the hot blue flicker of a flame, burning my insides until a warm, achy feeling overtook me. Something I'd never experienced before, not even with Leo.

The color was startling against his golden features. Golden skin. Golden hair that reminded me of a field of golden wheat in the peak of the summer, right before fall hit and it was ready to harvest. His aristocratic nose would have had Prince William weeping with envy. And those lips...I knew a thousand women who would give their left ovaries...or both ovaries...to get a pair.

"I'm sorry, what did you say?" I asked, realizing that the beautiful stranger had just spoken.

He looked at me, amused and unimpressed at the same time.

I blushed furiously under his gaze, feeling like an errant school girl who'd never seen a man before.

I quickly yanked my gaze back to the offensive-looking shirt in front of me, wondering idly why this perfect creature would be wanting anything to do with this shirt.

"I was saying we seem to have the same taste in horrible clothing," he said with a practiced grin that melted my insides.

His accent was American, and the timber of his voice was like honey, like he'd been biologically made to attract a mate in any way possible.

I could only imagine his scent. I resisted the urge to lean forward and try and capture it.

That would be too much, right?

He looked amused again and I belatedly gestured to my ruined shirt, only then realizing that not only was it stained… It was also see-through. When I quickly crossed my arms in front of my chest to try to hide the fact that my nipples were standing at attention, I almost missed the flash of heat in his gaze, followed by a surprised expression that looked out of place on his face. I'm sure a guy like him had seen a million boobs.

And with that thought, I turned my attention back to the shirt, dismissing whatever errant thoughts I'd had about him.

But a piece of me wondered…could a man like him make me feel?

"I'm sorry if I offended you. I'm sure the shirt would look amazing on you," he said quickly, blinding me with another perfect grin.

"I know why I'm buying this blight of patriotism, but why are you?" I asked, examining the expensive-looking black dress shirt and slacks he was sporting, the dark color making his golden appearance even more noticeable.

He brushed his hand through his hair, almost sheepishly. "It's a thing I do. Well, a thing I collect," he explained. "I try to get a trashy t-shirt from every country I visit."

"How many do you have?" I asked, giggling at the thought of this veritable god having a closet somewhere stuffed with corny t-shirts. I tried picturing him in one, but my mind couldn't quite wrap around the thought.

He chuckled, probably at the look on my face. The sound

reverberated right through me, stoking the flames inside that I was trying desperately to suppress. I didn't want to jump the man after all, and I was really close to that.

"Fifty-three?" he mused, stroking his lips with his thumb as he thought about it...I found myself strangely jealous of that thumb. "Well, I guess fifty-four as soon as this piece of art is paid for."

"Well, your reason for buying this shirt is far better than my clumsiness."

I rifled through the shirts, looking for my size. Once I found it, I turned around and almost dropped it when I found him staring at me intensely, all the earlier lightheartedness completely gone. He was studying me closely...clinically, like he was tearing off the layers of my skin to see what was inside.

I hoped he didn't venture too far down, he would only be disappointed when he got to my insides and found there was nothing but empty space.

What did it say about me that this small glimpse of the darker side of him only made me more attracted?

"Well," I began awkwardly. "Enjoy your shirt," I finished lamely, wanting to slap myself in the face for not being able to come up with something wittier.

"I hope you can find another coffee before your flight," he said charmingly as he reached past me and began to look through the shirts.

I was far more reluctant to leave his side than I would've liked as I headed towards the cashier stand to pay for my shirt. The bored-looking clerk quickly rang up my purchase, snapping her gum loudly as she did so. I forced myself not to wince. I'd always hated the sound of chewing. Chewing gum. Chewing food. It all drove me mad. Just another one of the little idiosyncrasies that set me apart from the rest of society.

I grabbed the shirt, not bothering to have her bag it since I would just be putting it on, and strode towards the exit, furtively looking around to see if I could get one more glimpse of him. He was still by the shirts, and he didn't turn around when I strode past him.

That was really okay, though; the backside of him was almost as good as the front.

As soon as I stepped out of the store, it all came rushing back. Where I was going. The fact that technically I was an engaged woman… It would take a minute to get used to that. I waited for the rush of guilt to hit me, since I'd spent the last two weeks after finding out about this whole arranged marriage trying to wrap my mind around the idea of becoming a stranger's wife.

Nope. Nothing. Not a flicker of guilt that I was just lusting crazily over a stranger.

My mum would be so disappointed, God bless her distracted, oblivious soul.

Rosemary Butcher was a lot of things, but oblivious was probably the most apt description for her. Oblivious to my father's sins, oblivious to my brothers following in his footsteps, oblivious to her daughter's pain.

I stepped into the bathroom stall, thinking of how excited she'd been for me as we said our farewells. She'd thought that this was the most amazing thing that could have happened to me. It would've been amazing if she was actually right.

But Rosemary Butcher was never right.

About anything.

I shook my head and pulled off my blouse, trying to push away the memory of that last hug she'd given me before she'd "spotted out for tea." It was amazing how someone could love you so much, and at the same time, not see you at all.

I should've just stuffed my shirt in my bag. I'm sure someone could have gotten the stain out, but instead, I impulsively threw it into a trashcan in the stall. I tore off the tag to the Union Jack shirt and slipped it on, immediately realizing that I'd somehow managed to get a size too small. I blamed it on being distracted and cringed as I pictured showing up to New York in a skin-tight t-shirt sporting the Union Jack flag.

Deciding I didn't have a choice but to buy another size, I peered into the trashcan to see if I could grab my blouse so I could take this one off and exchange it.

Of course, I muttered to myself, when I saw that I'd managed to throw the blouse right into an open diaper filled with poop.

I guess I was about to be the proud owner of *two* Union Jack shirts. Maybe there were better ones in there that I could find.

CHAPTER 2

As soon as I stepped out of the bathroom, an announcement blared out from above me that "flight 41182 to JFK" was about to board.

Nausea burst into play inside of me. The butterflies from earlier turned into veritable fireworks, threatening to send the sandwich I'd eaten an hour before all over the floor.

I looked longingly towards the store, a part of me obviously noting that the scorching hot stranger I'd met there wasn't inside, and then I hustled to my gate like the good girl I was.

I probably had time, but since this was my first time traveling commercial, I didn't want to risk it. I had no idea how much time there was between announcements like that and the plane actually taking off.

I sighed in relief…or misery, when I saw that the gate doors were indeed still open, and there was a line in front of them to get on the plane. I double-checked that my tickets were still in my bag. Looking around, I saw that everyone else had their tickets on their phone, but I was terrible at technology, and it felt much safer to have tangible tickets rather than something on my phone that could disappear with my clumsy fumbling.

Plus, I wasn't quite sure that the paper tickets would work on my phone.

Part of being a member of *The Firm* meant that there were a million firewalls on my phone to prevent hacking—not that there was actually anything interesting on my phone to be hacked. Pa had always gone on and on about security though.

My thoughts scattered as the line moved forward, and then it was my turn to give the tickets to the gate agent. My hand was trembling as I handed her the tickets, but she didn't say anything. She just shot me a polite, tight smile and nodded at the guest behind me to hand her their tickets. I rolled my shoulders back, becoming aware once again of just how tightly the shirt stretched across my chest, and started down the gangway…or at least I think that's what it was called.

The walk felt a mile long. I wondered if that's how prisoners felt when they were walking the plank—that it stretched on for miles…yet wasn't long enough.

Except then I thought about what I was leaving behind, and some of my anxiety disappeared. Every step meant I was farther from *him*. And even though my brother, Benny, had cast my uncle out as soon as my father died, for reasons unrelated to me, in my head he was still right behind me.

My fingers itched for a razor-blade at the thought.

I don't do that anymore, I reminded myself as I finally got to the entrance of the plane and stepped inside. That was another part of my fresh start. I didn't make myself bleed so I could stop feeling.

I wondered how long it would take to not crave the feeling of release as dear to me as water was to a desperate man.

There was a smiling flight attendant at the entrance handing out antiseptic packets, and I nodded my thanks as I took one. I wondered what I looked like to her. If I appeared as pale and out of sorts as I felt. Or if I just looked daft.

"I like your shirt," she said with a smile and an American accent. Which of course made me immediately think of the stranger in the store. There had been a few American students at my boarding school, and I'd always been fascinated by their accents…as fascinated as they were with mine.

I smiled in response, knowing she really didn't mean it—because really, who would?—and I turned to go farther into the plane. My jaw dropped. I was sure that this airline was far nicer than most because the first-class cabin had what looked like little square pods lined up down the aisle. I could see the tops of people's heads and not much else inside of them. I'd been imagining myself squished in a middle seat like in the movies with some drunk guy leaning his head on mine and snoring loudly as he drooled.

At least I would have some privacy. My rich mafia boss fiancé had sprung for first-class…the gentleman. Excuse my sarcasm.

I examined my ticket then started to scan the seats for 10C. Someone bumped me from behind, obviously not believing in personal space, and I walked a little bit faster down the row.

From this angle, I could see into most of the seats as I passed, since most people hadn't put up their privacy screens yet. The brown leather seats matched the outside of the pod and were at least three people wide. There was a tray off to the side and tons of space in front of the seat, I assumed so you could make the seat into a bed. Flight attendants were walking along the rows of first-class with trays laden with bubbly-filled glasses.

Getting drunk sounded good about now.

I found 10C and slid in gratefully, tossing my bag to the

ground with a sigh and sinking back into the surprisingly comfortable seats.

"It'll do for eight hours," a familiar voice commented from next to me, and I shot up in my seat, heat flushing through me as the screen separating me from the pod next to me slid down.

It was him. The beautiful stranger from the shop.

Maybe the heavens really did love me. Or they hated me. I guess I would find out in the next eight hours as I did my best to shield this guy from the full force of my awkwardness…and darkness.

Not that I assumed he would want to talk to me for eight hours. If anything, having him next to me would distract me from what awaited me at the end of the flight.

10C was located in the center of the plane. The seats on the sides of the plane were solo seats not connected to anyone else, but the ones in the center of the plane were side by side with another pod.

Not that I was complaining.

"You're not much of a talker, I take it," he commented, breaking me out of my head where I seemed to spend most of my time.

"I'm a talker. I love to talk," I spit out, wanting to find the nearest acid bath and jump in as soon as my word vomit came out.

He didn't seem to be put off. Instead, he leaned forward over the partition. "Well, that's good to know. I wouldn't want to have to sit the whole flight in silence." He winked at me, and I swore that my knickers melted. They just melted right off. I bet if I looked at the ground, there would just be a puddle of melted fabric.

I resisted the urge to take a look.

"So, is New York your final destination?" he asked, clearly better at conversing than I was.

"Yes. New York's going to be my new home, actually."

He smirked at that answer, like it delighted him or something.

"Do you live in New York?" I asked, not sure if I wanted him to answer yes. I didn't even know what my new husband looked like. Although I'd been assured by my brother Benny that "he didn't resemble an arsehole" and he wasn't an old man, I was still picturing a decrepit man in a wheelchair a la Anna Nicole Smith.

It might be torture to know that the Adonis next to me was walking the streets in the same city where I lived.

Don't get me wrong, I'd tried to find pictures of Lucian Rossi aka the future "Boss" of the famed Cosa Nostra, but he'd somehow had zero web presence. No Facebook. No Instagram. No TikTok. I'd found one mention of someone at a society event with his name, but of course, there was no picture attached.

"Yes. I've lived there my whole life, actually," he answered, doing that thing where he brushed his lips with his thumb. He was studying me again, and I once more had the urge to put on extra layers of clothing…just so he wouldn't find me lacking…or find out the truth.

"Champagne?" a flight attendant asked from next to me, making me jump in my seat as she pulled me from whatever spell my seat neighbor had weaved around me.

"Yes, please," I murmured as she handed me a glass. I took a big gulp, trying not to choke on the bubbles.

"Sir?" she whispered in a voice that had somehow transformed from the professional tone she'd used for me into one that would suit her well if she was a phone sex operator.

Jealousy clawed at my insides, and I frowned at myself for being so weirdly proprietary about a man I didn't even know.

I didn't get jealous. Leo had tried that in an effort to get me to care, but he'd soon learned that I just didn't. I didn't get attached. I didn't get upset. And I didn't cry.

So, this was new.

"Why not?" he answered with a wink so sexy that I swore I heard a soft moan come from the flight attendant's lips.

Hussy.

He took the flute from her, and I cocked my head as I studied his movements. The practiced, charming smile was there, but there was a certain blankness in his eyes as he thanked the woman. It wasn't the warm look he gave me, not even the cold one I'd witnessed for a brief moment in the store.

It was just blank…

Intriguing.

She didn't seem to notice, judging by the way she was panting next to me.

I took a moment to check my phone while she tried to small talk him over my head.

I miss you.

Leo's text should have done something to me, given me a pang of longing…regret. But I'd just used him as a distraction. A place to lay my lips for a moment when the memories became too much. He was a fool for believing it was anything more.

I didn't answer his message, and after checking to make sure there wasn't anything from my mum, or my brothers… which there wasn't, I threw my phone in my bag.

An announcement rang through the cabin, and the Captain began speaking, forcing the flight attendant to drag herself away from my side as she moved to ready the cabin.

I was sure that she'd be back as often as possible.

"Why the move?" he commented, dragging my attention back to his face.

I opened my mouth, but the words I should have said didn't come out. "Just needed a change," I answered, and his eyes glimmered as if my vague answer amused him.

"We all do sometimes," he responded, once again brushing his lips with his thumb. This close up, his lips looked so soft. I wondered if they would feel that soft against mine.

The plane began to move then, and I gripped the edge of my seat, working to relax myself as I prepared for takeoff. I let go of the seat long enough to drain the rest of the champagne that I'd set on the side tray. I set the flute down sharply as the plane began to pick up speed.

"Not a fan of flying?" he asked, his hand reaching over to brush mine.

"I love flying, actually," I whispered, the plane shaking as it raced forward. "It's just the takeoff I hate."

His fingertips brushed soothingly against my arm

"What's your name?" I asked in a choked voice, figuring that I should probably get his name at this point, since he was touching me…

Not that I minded his touch. The surprising roughness of his fingers was doing a nice job of distracting me. A more sane person probably would have politely pulled away, but I'd learned early on in life I was far from sane.

"Raphael," he said softly. I found myself smiling even though the plane was taking off…because of course he would be named after an angel. It was the most fitting name I'd ever heard for a person.

"You're laughing at me," he mused as his fingers kept up their maddening stroke across my skin.

"Just a little," I giggled a little crazily.

"Evidently, I came out with a full head of blonde hair. It

was sticking straight up. My mother inanely thought it looked like an angel's halo, hence Raphael." He shook his head, "Mothers do seem to do that, don't they? Romanticize their young." Raphael smiled, but it looked a little pained.

"You say that like it's a bad thing."

"It's just an amusing thing that we do as a society, give our children names at birth when we have no idea who they'll become," he responded.

I cocked my head at his statement, the takeoff completely forgotten. "I've never really thought about that."

"I've shown you mine, now you show me yours," he said.

"What?"

"Your name. I don't believe I've gotten that yet."

"Dahlia," I answered, a faint flush rising on my cheeks. For some reason, it seemed intimate to give him my name, even though that was the normal thing that people did.

"Any story behind that?"

"My mum was a romantic as well," I said with a laugh. "She grew up on a farm in Lacock...that's a blink and miss town in southern England if you didn't know...and evidently there were flowers everywhere. Dahlias." I shrugged. "It's not a very interesting story."

"I like it," he answered, and I realized that he was still touching my arm.

He must have realized the same thing because he withdrew his hand, reluctantly it seemed. Or I was probably imagining that.

"Oh, look, we're in the air," he announced, turning his head to try and see out the window.

The plane had leveled, and I'd escaped the usual fifteen minutes of terror. "Thank you for the distraction," I smiled.

He laughed, and I about died from the sound of it.

The next hour passed quickly. We talked about football—

European football, that is—and I found out that he actually knew a little about the game.

"Chelsea till I die," I argued with a laugh as he tried to convince me that Real Madrid was where my heart should lie.

"You'll have to go to a Giant's game," he told me. "I have season tickets in a suite."

My heart fluttered…it almost sounded like he was planning…a date.

Which would have been a dream—if I wasn't about to be a married woman.

"Did I say something wrong?" he asked.

I just shook my head, my stomach clenching. I was good at that, disassociating so I could forget hard truths.

But they were always waiting for me.

"No, sometimes I do that, get lost in my head," I answered sheepishly.

"So, is there a boyfriend back home?" he asked. I fiddled with the blanket that one of the flight attendants had just dropped off.

"Why do you ask?" I answered.

"Ahh, so there is someone special. I knew an English rose like you wouldn't be unattached." His hand was touching my arm again, and I swear I was feeling drunk from it.

English rose. I'd heard that a lot, that my name should have been Rose instead of Dahlia. I was delicate looking, with blonde hair and blue eyes, and lips that were cartoonishly large in my opinion. I had similar coloring to Raphael, but somehow my features didn't add up to the brilliant package that he was blessed with.

I'd secretly always liked my name, even if it didn't fit my appearance. Dahlias were unexpected. They came in so many different colors and sizes that half the time the gardener had no idea what was going to spring up when they planted one.

People would probably find a lot of things surprising about me if they could see behind the mask I perpetually wore.

I thought about his statement...that I had someone special.

I most assuredly did not. A future mafia boss and a Uni boy-child most assuredly did not count as special.

"There's no one, actually," I said defensively, as if I was trying to convince myself. "You?"

The cabin lights dimmed just then. The flight was a red-eye. We'd land around 4:00 pm in New York with the time change, so I assumed that most of the passengers were going to sleep.

"I'm excruciatingly single," he announced.

"Excruciatingly? Not a fan of playing the field, then?"

He smirked as if he knew a joke I wasn't in on.

"I have a difficult time forming attachments. Or maybe the right girl just hasn't come around yet."

The way he said it was like he was hinting that he thought I could be the right girl.

Which obviously was just my wistful, wishful thinking since he didn't even know me.

He didn't seem to care that I was tongue-tied. "Are you tired, or do you want to watch a movie? This barrier goes down all the way. It's usually reserved for couples so they can have little rooms to themselves on the flight. We could watch a movie until they bring by some food."

I flushed, hoping that the dim lighting of the cabin hid my blush at least a little bit.

Was I going to do this? This was decidedly very non-good girl behavior.

"I'm just going to use the loo, and then that sounds lovely," I told him, getting up from my seat and trying to hide the fact that my hands were shaking. I also needed a minute to get over the fact I'd actually just said something as asinine like "that sounds lovely" to the hottest man I'd ever seen.

"Have fun in the "loo"," he teased, and I flushed more, remembering that Americans used terms like restroom and bathroom.

I rolled my eyes and hurried away.

Continue Dahlia's story: books2read.com/ruiningdahlia

JOIN C.R.'S FATED REALM

Visit my **Facebook** page to get updates.

Visit my **Amazon Author** page.

Visit my website at www.crjanebooks.com

Sign up for my **newsletter** to stay updated on new releases, find out random facts about me, and get access to different points of view from my characters.

BOOKS BY C.R. JANE

www.crjanebooks.com

The Sounds of Us Contemporary Series (complete series)

Remember Us This Way

Remember You This Way

Remember Me This Way

Broken Hearts Academy Series: A Bully Romance (complete duet)

Heartbreak Prince

Heartbreak Lover

Ruining Dahlia (Contemporary Mafia Standalone)

Ruining Dahlia

The Fated Wings Series (Paranormal series)

First Impressions

Forgotten Specters

The Fallen One (a Fated Wings Novella)

Forbidden Queens

Frightful Beginnings (a Fated Wings Short Story)

Faded Realms

Faithless Dreams

Fabled Kingdoms

Fated Wings 8

The Rock God (a Fated Wings Novella)

Sweet Destiny

Kingdom of Wolves Co-write with Mila Young

Wild Moon

Wild Heart

Wild Girl

Wild Love

Wild Soul

Stupid Boys Series Co-write with Rebecca Royce

Stupid Boys

Dumb Girl

Crazy Love

Breathe Me Duet Co-write with Ivy Fox (complete)

Breathe Me

Breathe You

Rich Demons of Darkwood Series Co-write with May Dawson

Make Me Lie

Make Me Beg

Make Me Wild

Printed in Great Britain
by Amazon